SHIFTER MOUNTAIN

HEARTS OF STONE

BOOK ONE

Shifter Mountain

Hearts Of Stone

Book One

ISBN: 978-1-77357-328-1

978-1-77357-327-4

Published by Naughty Nights Press LLC

Cover Design by C.D. Gorri

Proofread by: Book Nook Nuts

DEDICATION

To Jason, thanks for all the support and encouragement!

SHIFTER MOUNTAIN

Even the hardest heart has its weakness.

Keeton Grey is an Eastern Mountain Lion Shifter with a serious people problem. As in, he hates all of them. Betrayal is a bitter pill to swallow for most, but for Keeton, it's damn near impossible. Choosing to live in seclusion, he finds his peace of mind disrupted when an injured hiker stumbles onto his property.

After she catches her fiancé cheating, Marilena Sorelli needs a break from life. Not much of an outdoor girl, hiking alone proves unwise after Lena takes a serious tumble. She meets her rescuer in a nearly seven-foot-tall giant with piercing green eyes and a beard that makes her fingers itch to run through it. Will the beautiful interloper crack this rugged Shifter's heart of stone, or will self-imposed isolation be his future?

PROLOGUE

KEETON'S MOUNTAIN LION hissed angrily as he boarded the plane for the States. Three months on Moongate Island did nothing to repair his faith in people. Shifter or human, they pretty much sucked.

True, he was no longer being

blackmailed by the sniveling cretin who'd been part of his last black ops assignment. Fucker had stepped on a landmine deep in the jungles of a place Keeton was not at liberty to name. Not even in his own head.

Fucking hell.

Yeah, it meant he could return home now, but to who? Keeton had no family waiting for him. His few friends were back on the island, but that was no place for his inner feline. The beast craved the hills and valleys of the New Jersey forests he called home.

He'd bought a hundred acres of forest off the beaten paths of New Jersey's Panther Mountains years ago. Even commissioned the building of a cabin deep in the woods. The design was environmentally conscientious and entirely sound. Two stories high, it had its own generators, additional solar paneling, and wind turbines for power, and indoor plumbing.

He wasn't an animal, for fuck's sake. But even if Keeton was going to avoid people, he didn't have to be uncomfortable doing it. Eyes closed, he sat seemingly at ease, but he was keeping tabs on every living thing around him on the plane.

Once a soldier, always a soldier, his two commanders, Callan McGregor and Landry Smyth, had said that often enough. Both men were Shifters, a unique Alpha and Omega pair who'd completed their Triad once they'd found their mate in Sage Freeman, a smart mouthed human female. That had been Keeton's cue to leave the island he'd called home for eighty-nine and a half days.

They hadn't kicked him out or anything. On the contrary. But he was restless and antsy. The island could no longer contain his need for isolation.

Memories of the disgust on Bruce Taylor's face when he'd seen Keeton lose control of his shift during a particularly bloody battle were forever ingrained in his brain. The human male had been a new recruit in the special ops task force where Keeton had served his country for the last five years in secret.

Dismantling dictatorships and stopping atrocities the likes of which he could hardly put a name to before they could ever see the light of day had been his job, and blackmail was his reward.

He'd kept the fact that he'd unwittingly told the secret about Shifters to the human from Callan and Landry until the night Bruce had died believing Keeton was the only one of his kind. The two men had investigated his claims, making sure that he never downloaded or emailed the proof he'd recorded with his phone the night Keeton lost control.

The half a million dollars he'd sent to Bruce's offshore bank was nothing. He didn't care about the money. It was simply the point of it all. The man had not trusted Keeton because of his dual nature. And he'd lost his life as a result.

"We need to stick to this route, Bruce,"

he growled at the human who'd become increasingly toxic to their two-man operation.

"Think I'm gonna trust a fucking animal. I'll go this way," the man argued.

After a few more minutes of trying to convince him, Keeton threw his hands up. His beast scratched at his skin, the animal sensing something was not right. The sounds of the explosion and Bruce's bitter cry rang in his ears, but he died before Keeton could ever hope to reach him.

It was his fault. He was the reason Bruce had died. After pledging his life to help save lives, he'd brought death instead.

Keeton was better off on his own.

CHAPTER ONE

WHAT THE ACTUAL fuck?

Lena sat behind the wheel of her SUV in the now filthy wedding dress she'd so lovingly bought in utter and complete shock.

Was this real life?

Like, did that actually just happen?

She looked up and squinted at the bright headlights from the oncoming traffic, trying desperately to shield her vision from their halogen glares. What the hell was she doing sitting outside with her trunk full of her still-packed suitcases and garbage bags of clothing and other random doohickeys and knick-knacks she grabbed before hightailing it out of there? Most of her furniture and things were still in storage.

Thank God for small favors, she thought. But seriously. How the hell had she wound up here? She retraced her steps in her mind and was no closer to an answer. After all, she did everything right. She'd started a business and was finally making a profit. Lena had found the right sort of guy and even gotten him to propose.

Cary was a lawyer. Smart as a whip and a real smooth talker. She'd agreed to go out with him immediately, flattered as she was by the tall, slender blond's attentions. Hell, she'd even given up carbs for the fucker. He'd insisted her weight was a negative reflection on him, and he was up for partner. Had to make a good impression.

After he'd proposed and laid out his plans to "fix" her, Marilena had simply smiled and agreed. Her mother told her for years she was too chubby to appeal to any man. At the time, Lena had simply ignored her. She'd always relied on her brains and optimism to get her through the tough times, but the truth was she'd always been a bigger girl.

She was a chef, for fuck's sake. Food was a lot like life. It could be vibrant and fun, but there were consequences. Such as those to her hips and belly from a love of all things chocolate.

Sigh.

Still, she tried. For Cary and for her mother. Yes, Marilena loved blending cuisines from all over the world to create tempting and tasty treats her customers loved for their parties and events. She worked damn hard at it too, despite her mother's criticisms. For some reason, her trim parent thought fat equaled lazy.

But Lena was not lazy. She'd even agreed to Cary's demands to work out five times a week, despite not losing a single pound over the last few months of killing herself. She enjoyed exercise, chub and all, but honestly, she preferred nature walks to spin class.

"I don't have time to go hiking with you," Cary said every time she brought it up.

"Okay, dear," was her only reply.

And yet, it wasn't enough. Nothing she did or sacrificed was enough for the golden fiancé she'd been so proud to bring home to her disbelieving mother. That same parent who'd refused to let her come home tonight, insisting she apologize to that scoundrel.

"Try to work things out, Lena. Who else is gonna want you?"

Imagine that? Lena apologizing for Cary sticking his dick in another woman. Ha! That would be the day. Her mind wandered to the events that led to her pulling up at the Oasis Beachside Resort down in Maccon City.

The Jersey shore town had been her home away from home during college. She'd always felt good there. Accepted. Even lusted after by the many handsome locals. And that was something out of the ordinary for all her experience during her years in culinary school in Connecticut. But back to her reality as of a few hours ago.

Marilena Sorelli walked into the apartment she shared with her fiancé on her tiptoes. She was so excited to surprise Cary. Switching her flight to the redeye, just so she could show him the incredible gown she'd bought while she was away, had taken most of her savings, but it was worth it.

Her fiancé was overly concerned about her weight. Especially with their upcoming nuptials, and she really couldn't blame him. Lena was a size sixteen on a good day, but try as she might, there were some things she could not lose. Like her thick thighs, big butt, and larger than average breasts. Go figure she'd go for a guy who wanted runway model thin in his significant other.

But he'd asked her to marry him, so she must mean something to him. Right? She was determined to make Cary happy. Luckily, the Las Vegas Foodie Con she'd attended, hoping to learn how to expand her catering business, was also home to a famous plus-size designer whose gowns were to die for.

She was so lucky to run into Ava Marrow in the lobby of her hotel. The vivacious woman had agreed to see her last minute, claiming she had the perfect dress for Lena's figure. And boy, did she ever!

The gown was incredible. Marilena looked fabulous in it if she said so herself. Yes, she knew it was bad luck for the groom to see the bride in her dress before the wedding, but that was just an old superstition!

Slipping inside the door, she stripped out of her travel clothes and donned the dress, hoping to catch Cary as he woke up. He was a real stickler for schedules and insisted the alarm be set for the same time every single day. Weekends too.

While she expected the chimes of the antiquated alarm clock, she did not expect the sight that greeted her when she walked into the room.

There he was. Her neat as a pin, perfectly poised, and often boring if she were being honest, fiancé. He was laying in the middle of their king-sized bed with a bucket of ice holding an empty bottle of champagne, a dish of strawberry stems, and Dawn. His stick-figure secretary.

"Are you fucking kidding me? You had food in bed?"

Lena's shriek of outrage over the fact that he'd fed his other woman a bowl of plump strawberries in bed when he freaked out if she so much as drank water while sitting beneath the covers might have seemed irrelevant. But it was all in the details. Which was why, after she caught the two of them *in flagrante delicto,* she grabbed the bucket of ice and upended it over Cary's cheating head.

A few choice words, and okay, yes, she might have tossed the bowl of strawberries at him as well while Dawn went running for cover.

"Lena! I thought you weren't coming home 'till this afternoon," he yelled while she hurled strawberries, crackers, and the bottle of spray cheese the SOB had been feasting on at his head.

"I wasn't you, big jerk!"

"Dawn and I just happened, it wasn't planned. You are being unreasonable—"

"I'm being unreasonable? You had your dick in another woman, Cary. I don't think I'm unreasonable. Goodbye."

"You can't do this! What will the partners think?"

"Honestly, Cary, I don't give two shits what they or you think. It's over."

She'd tossed his ring at his head, grabbed whatever she could, then left. Filling her trunk and pulling over on the side of the road to call her mother, whose only response was that Lena shouldn't have surprised him.

Sigh.

Thank goodness the motel had a vacancy. She wiped her face as best she could, grabbed her suitcase, and checked in.

"One room, Miss Sorelli?" Joelle

Flint, Manager, her nametag read, furrowed her dark eyebrows as she handed Lena her key.

She was young and sweet, Lena thought as she signed the credit card slip. The woman did not mention Lena's current state. Or the fact she was wearing a strapless wedding dress at ten o'clock in the morning in late Autumn in New Jersey and had obviously been crying.

"Hey, is everything alright?"

"Yes," Lena said and sniffed softly. "Well, I mean, I just dumped my lying, cheating fiancé. My mother thinks I should apologize to him, and I hung up on her for the first time in ever. All my stuff is in storage. And I have no idea what I am going to do. But I am okay. I think."

Her smile faltered, but that didn't stop the young woman from coming around to the front of the desk. She took one look at Lena, then wrapped her up in a surprisingly strong and quick embrace.

"You look like you needed that," Joelle said, and Lena couldn't stop a sob from escaping her lips.

"Sorry," she said, trying to stem the flow of tears that fell even faster.

"It's okay, really. Now, I don't recall my mother because she and my dad died when I was young, so, I really don't know what one is supposed to act like, but I can guarantee from the way my sister Maggie raised me, that your mother sucks."

"Ha! She does," Lena replied, laughing through her tears.

"Look, I can tell you're a good person, and this guy, hell, you're better off without the rat!"

"Thank you. Truth is, I feel kind of relieved," she whispered her secret and covered her mouth immediately.

Oh, my!

Did she really just say that?

And worse, did she mean it?

Yes. She did. Her eyes widened at the truth behind those words.

"Sister, I don't blame you one bit," Joelle replied, smirking as she handed Lena her key card. "Will there be anything else?"

"Yes," Lena thought, her gaze roaming around until it landed on a stack of shiny new brochures.

"May I please have one of those pamphlets for Panther Mountains?"

"Of course. You know, there are some lovely trails there this time of year. The foliage is beautiful."

"I bet."

"Here you go," Joelle said, handing her the tri-fold paper. "You're gonna be okay, Marilena Sorelli."

"You know, something? I think, I am."

CHAPTER TWO

WHAT THE ACTUAL fuck?

Keeton stalked through the woods, feline senses on high alert. The sounds of soft whimpers and bitten back moans reached his sensitive ears. This patch of forest high in the Panther Mountains was his domain.

My territory.

His Mountain Lion snarled loudly. The sound caused the source of those devilishly intriguing noises to stifle a gasp. He wanted to laugh, would have if he wore skin and not fur, but regardless of the person's attempts to quiet themselves, Keeton was very much aware of their presence.

The notes in the air turned sour with fear and he puffed out a breath, scrunching his feline nose in distaste. Lemony tart was not his favorite flavor. He was more a rosewater and honey type Mountain Lion. Aptly named the ghost cat, Keeton crept forward. Really, he should just roar and scare the piss out of the trespasser, but something elusive about the man held his interest.

Unable to resist, he snarled once more, even louder than before. The stranger yelped, then gasped again, as if the sudden movement jarred something out of place. Whatever. A man could crawl with a broken leg. He'd seen it often enough when he'd been on active duty. He listened for the rustle of leaves, nodded satisfactorily as the interloper started moving off his property. Then *crash*, *boom*, *thud*, and more whimpering.

Hmmpf.

Served the ingrate right. Keeton would harbor no intruders in his inner sanctum. He sniffed the air, hissing at the decidedly human scent that reached him. But where he expected some hot shot male foolish enough to walk onto his property despite the warning signs, he'd posted every hundred yards since his return to US Soil, the floral notes on the air told him it was a woman who dared invade his domain. A woman who he was fairly sure had injured herself on the rocks hidden beneath the layers of slippery leaves that had fallen between bouts of rain the last week or so.

Shit.

He couldn't leave a woman out there all night. The sun would set soon, and he still had to go back for his change of clothes before he could let her see him. First, he'd better make sure she was not in any real danger.

He leapt onto a sturdy limb from a nearby birch tree. Creeping forward stealthily, Keeton balanced his long, muscular body on the branch that dangled over the rocky patch of ground the woman had stumbled upon. Hair the color of a desert sunset, a sort of rusty gold caught his eye, but that wasn't the only thing about her that dazzled.

The female wore a pair of well-worn jeans that hugged her curvy frame. She was leaning over a backpack, its contents now spilled across the forest floor, and she tried earnestly to gather them up silently. From what he could see she had a toothbrush, shampoo, some clothes, bug spray, and fuck, was that a taser gun?

She was completely adorable. Everything inside of him swelled with the need to go to her. To make sure she was unhurt, keep her safe from harm. Once she had her belongings, he feared he missed his chance. But the sweet looking woman bit her lip and cried out as her ankle refused to support her, and she slumped back to her knees.

Grrr.

He fought his cat's urge to run to her, turning back instead for the nearest of his secret stashes of clothes spread throughout the mountains. He would give her the aid she required, but he needed to be dressed to do that.

The sooner he helped her, the sooner she would be gone. Off his property. Out of his life. Then Keeton wouldn't have to worry about the very real dangers she posed to his lifestyle. No, he wouldn't think about that now. Refused to even say it aloud.

He shrugged on his jeans and flannel, using his long stride to his advantage just in case she managed to try to wander off. Foolish woman could get herself really hurt. True, he was the fiercest beast in the land, but not the only one. There were plenty of black bears, a few wolves, and several coyotes in the Panther Mountains.

Wild creatures who were generally wary of his turf, but the area she'd fallen was near the edge of his territory. There was no telling who or what she'd run into if he didn't get to her in time.

Keeton inhaled a deep breath, picking up the floral hints of the female's scent along with the distinct tartness of fear. His Mountain Lion roared inside of him. The beast didn't want the woman scared. He pressed against his skin, scratching, and clawing for Keeton to move faster. He didn't want to startle her any further, so he purposely made noise, changing his stealthy animalistic tread for that of his noisier, less graceful half.

"Hello? Is someone there?" she cried out, and her husky voice was like a balm to his soul.

Grrr.

Keeton paused, allowing the dulcet tones to wash over him. Something was different about this woman. Sure, he had his fair share of trysts. Nothing but bodies in the dark to satisfy an itch, a natural urge he could no more control than he could his need to shift.

He should not think such thoughts. Could not afford to even imagine indulging in the seductive female who needed his help. No. He would simply walk her back to her camp. She must have come on a tour or some such thing. They were frequent this time of year, but never came this far out.

He should know, having spent the last eighteen months alone in his cabin. No one for miles except the occasional hikers who wandered too far from civilization to prove something to themselves. Keeton had no time for those people. No time for liars and fools.

She's neither, his beast whispered insistently in his mind's eye. But he refused to heed the animal. Just as he refused to acknowledge the hardness in his jeans at the sight of her soft, flushed skin when he made himself known.

"Oh! You scared me." She laid a hand over her chest and closed her eyes, relief easing her muscles.

He wondered what she would do if he told her. He was the most dangerous thing out there. Cocking his head to the side, he watched as she struggled to stand. Not quite trusting himself to touch her just yet. His Lion was far too close to the surface for that.

"I'm so glad you're here. I twisted my dang ankle," she said, still talking although he hadn't uttered a word. "And I think I heard a bear or something just a little while ago. Damn near peed my pants."

The strange woman exhaled a breath

and leaned over to grab her bulky backpack. She shouldn't try that on such slippery terrain, but before he could utter a warning, she was halfway to tipping over and landing on that gorgeous rump of hers.

Shit.

He darted forward on sure feet. Never had a problem with the leaves and rocks himself, but he was a Shifter, and this was his territory. Keeton knew the terrain like the back of his hand.

"Oooh!"

"Here, I got you," he grunted, and the raspy sound of his voice surprised even his own ears.

The stranger looked up at him with enormous hazel eyes, the color of which he couldn't pin down. One moment green, the next russet, circled in black with flecks of gold throughout. He was hypnotized. Forgot he was holding her for a moment, but the feel of her soft, honey scented skin snug against his was enough to wake his innermost longings.

"Thank you," she whispered the words, the soft rustle like leaves in the wind.

Her voice had a calming effect on his Mountain Lion, but her ultra feminine body, well, that had the opposite effect on him. Too hastily, Keeton pushed away from her, causing the petite beauty to wobble unsteadily.

"Sorry," she murmured, clutching his flannel with her fingers.

He should've let her fall, but there

was no fucking way he'd do such a thing. He steadied her with firm hands, stepping back so as not to brush his suddenly rock hard cock against her softness. She was everything beautiful and bright that he'd forgotten about the world when he'd locked himself away in the mountains.

"I'm Marilena, but everyone calls me Lena for short. It's spelled L-E-N-A but pronounced *lay-nah*. Throws everyone, but my dad was Italian."

She shrugged and cleared her throat. Perhaps she was uncomfortable with silences, but Keeton had grown used to them. He simply watched as she bit her lower lip, releasing her hold on his shirt. She was still wobbly, so he held out his hand. An offering that she took with a grateful smile.

Keeton grunted indifferently, but it was a ruse. A storm of lightning like zings zipped up and down his body. Like electrical currents zapping him into awareness. He grabbed the backpack before she could reach for it once again, shrugging it onto his free shoulder while keeping a firm grip on her waist.

"Thanks," she repeated, but he couldn't talk just yet.

Keeton was trembling from head to toe. His heart was pounding so hard, he thought the blasted muscle was going to beat him to death.

What was she just talking about?

Her name?

Marilena.

Beautiful.

“Keeton!” He snapped. “What?” He closed his eyes and took a calming breath before turning their full force on her. Fuck, but she was so lovely. He pushed the Lion down, willing the creature to be still when he opened his mouth next to speak.

“My name is Keeton Grey.”

CHAPTER THREE

OH, MY.

Goodness gracious.

Sweet mercy.

Marilena was not exactly a nature girl. And yet, the second she'd seen the brochure in the hotel's lobby, the one she'd driven to after that disaster with

Cary, it was like she just knew. Like a big old neon arrow had pointed right at the glossy little thing saying, 'go on girl, this is your destiny'.

Well, her destiny had a completely fucked sense of humor. First off, chubby chicks did not dig walking for miles in the woods, uphill for fuck's sake, without her GPS. Yeah. Who knew? There were no cell towers in the Panther Mountains.

She should've known something was wrong when she'd stopped at the little mini mart before the trails began and the attendant had laughed at her when she told him which one, she was going to take.

"That's an expert trail, miss. Takes eight hours to get to the top and then you

gotta make camp. See how the dots on your map are red? Red means only hiking enthusiasts should attempt. You might wanna start with something more your speed. There, try the trail marked out in green on the other side of that map. That's the ticket for a city girl like you."

Next, the beady-eyed little cretin had pointed to a tiny circle marked out in green dots labeled appropriate for ages twelve and under. The jerk.

Hmmpf.

Nothing like throwing down a gauntlet to get Lena's panties in a bunch. Determined to prove even a fluffy girl like her could make it to the top of the expert trail, set up camp for the night, and start back down in the morning, she'd purchased a one-person tent, some protein bars, and extra waters, and started at daybreak.

Eight hours came more quickly than she thought, as her frequent stops made it difficult to keep to that time. But what could she say? Her need to pee won out more often than not. Even now she did not think she was anywhere near the campsite.

But the sun was already low in the afternoon sky and Lena was hungry, cold, and tired. She decided one wooded area was as good as another, but three strikes and she was too humiliated to try again. The first area she tried to pitch her tent was against a tree where some pretty angry squirrels were preparing for the coming winter.

Little buggers thought she was trying to steal their nuts and had retaliated by crawling up her thigh and chittering like mad. Lena had dropped to the floor and rolled to get the beasties off, but dang, they sure were feisty.

The second effort had resulted in her pushing a stake through a fire ant mound beneath a pile of leaves. Again, she went running for the hills. Literally.

After another twenty minutes of walking, Lena finally tried her latest attempt. Panther Mountain was so beautiful and peaceful. She knew it was a series of mountains, but still called it in the singular as the locals did. The storekeeper hadn't been wrong when he'd said the trail she'd chosen was for experts, but she couldn't let the mountain beat her. And she sure as hell wasn't about to let another man tell her what to do with her life.

Yes, she'd been foolish, but she could survive a night under the stars. This was her opportunity to spend some time alone with her thoughts. After countless hours of going through what she'd walked in on just a few days ago, Lena still felt one thing above all the betrayal and anger. Relief.

It was simple as that. Marrying Cary would have been a terrible mistake. He was the only one of her boyfriends her mother had ever liked. That alone should have been a red flag. She grinned at the thought and shook her head, searching for a clearing between the ever-thickening forest. The aches in her muscles now went all the way down to her bones. She had to rest for the night.

There'd been a few signs hanging up, claiming this section of woods was private property, but Lena saw no such details in her map. It was probably some kids playing pranks. So, she'd gone through a dense stand of tall pines and found paradise. A clearing. One that looked peaceful under the faint light from the rising moon glowing overhead.

Of course, slipping on the damp rocks hidden beneath the fallen Autumn leaves and spraining her dang ankle was not high on her list, but it happened. But what had she expected with her luck? Just when she thought all was lost, with the sky darkening and the sounds of roaming animals approaching, *he* showed up.

The man was a mountain himself. He was a giant, for sure. The tallest, widest human being Lena had ever seen. Her heart skipped two beats at his silent approach. For a moment, she'd thought she'd dreamed him up.

"Oh! You scared me," she'd said.

Then after that, she damn near talked his head off. Lena babbled when she was nervous, and Mr. Tall-Dark-and-Sexy made her nervous as hell. His eyes sparkled like green emeralds, his hands were big and sure as he steadied her when she almost tumbled head over teakettle once more.

If anyone could make a fool of

themselves at the most inopportune moments, it was her. So, grinning self-deprecatingly, she took his hand, grateful for the aid. He slipped a sure arm around her waist and shrugged her knapsack onto his back. Then he introduced himself.

"My name is Keeton."

Some things were coincidence, others were hard earned through work and years of searching. Then there were those things that the universe itself seemed to drop at your feet.

Like gifts, Lena often thought.

When Keeton said his name, she felt tiny sparks of electricity flit up and down her spine. Then her ankle rolled, but before she could go down like a ton of bricks, *or one large overly fluffy girl,* the mountain of a man swooped her into his arms before she even touched the ground. Lena had a moment of panic.

She didn't want him to carry her, to feel her weight so keenly. But he barely even slowed down. Walking at an unhurried pace while he held both her and her bag firmly in his firm grip. She'd never felt so small or protected before in her entire life. Maybe that was why instead of telling him to put her down, she simply wrapped her arms around his neck and held on.

"I have a cabin," he said in a deep, rumbling voice that did funny things to her insides.

The deep tones sort of turned her into a warm pile of goo. She nodded her head, swallowing the nerves that threatened to spill out. This was crazy.

He could be an axe murderer.

Or some crazy survivalist hiding from the government.

Or a ridiculously handsome man living alone on a mountain, starved for sex, and looking to scratch his itch with a chubby chick born and raised in Hoboken, New Jersey.

Gulp.

Before she could find her voice to ask for more information, they were there.

"Oh, wow!" Lena gasped as he carried her effortlessly along the cobblestoned walkway that led to an enormous two-story log cabin style house.

"When you said cabin, I thought you meant like a one room shack in the woods," she murmured.

"Why did you think that?" Keeton cocked his head to the side and looked curiously at her.

"Uh, I don't know. I think I can walk," she returned, a little embarrassed by both her supposition and the vulnerability she felt in his embrace.

It's not an embrace, Lena.

She scolded herself often whenever her flights of fancy were bound to get her into trouble. If she started thinking of this man in terms of embraces, Lena was liable to throw herself at him.

What kind of soul searching would she accomplish then when he laughed her right out of his beautiful home?

Sigh.

The sky opened up just as he

lowered her onto his covered porch, and Lena gasped, turning too quickly to see lightning crack through the suddenly black sky.

“Easy,” Keeton said, moving closer. His enormous body blocked Lena from getting wet by the raindrops that splattered on the rocks he’d used to decorate outside the cabin.

It was the perfect blend of wild and tamed. The building itself seemed more part of the landscape than she’d thought at first, and the result was beautiful.

“Come inside,” he said.

“Are you sure I won’t be intruding?”

“No,” his green eyes glowed as he spoke, and she swallowed at the pure turmoil she saw in them.

Something deep was going on with her reluctant host. An inner struggle she wasn't sure she was supposed to see. Common courtesy demanded she go find somewhere else to wait out the storm and call for aid, but Lena didn't have that luxury. She was stranded in the forest with no cell service, an injured ankle, and a thunderstorm raging. Keeton Grey was her only hope. And he wasn't done answering her, she realized when the hard line of his mouth opened once more.

"In fact, I'm positive you're intruding, Marilena Sorelli," he growled the words. "But come inside anyway."

CHAPTER FOUR

HEAVEN.

I am holding heaven in my arms, and it's sweet and soft, and fuck me, I don't deserve it.

Mine, his Mountain Lion chuffed happily with his mate in his arms.

Keeton had walked through the

familiar forest with the sweet smelling woman in his arms, and yes, he took the long way home just to prolong the contact. It was the most content he'd ever felt his inner beast.

It was slightly overwhelming to think a single female could render his powerful and solitary inner animal as docile as a fucking kitten. But there it was. The cat was purring, for fuck's sake. Lying belly up in that metaphysical plane where he dwelled until Keeton called his fur forward, deep within his mind's eye.

He'd never, ever seen the beast do that before. And it wasn't like there were other Eastern Mountain Lion Shifters around to help with this sort of thing. Loners in the wild, and unlike many other Shifter subspecies, his kind did not dwell in large groups or Prides. Fact was, there weren't very many of them around.

Occasionally, they teamed up with other Shifter groups, like he did with others in the military and after in the mercenary groups he worked for. Callan and Landry were an Alpha and Omega pair who'd allowed him to heal some with them on Moongate Island, and yes, it had helped his cat.

But the need to retreat from the world had been strong. His sense of betrayal too deep to rejoin humankind, he sought refuge here. The very last place he'd ever expected to run into a female, let alone his mate.

She was his. He knew it from the

moment he first caught her scent. But she was human. Knew nothing of Shifters and fated mates. And he was a fucking hermit. She'd be much better off without him.

Rrroooaaarrr!

His cat really did not like that thought. The beast scratched and clawed at him from the inside out, but he batted down the animal and turned to help the female hobble over to the sofa.

"I don't suppose you have a phone."

"Have a cell phone, but you can't get reception here."

"Then why do you have it?"

"There's a spot about eight miles down the trail you were on. I can get reception there when I need to."

"Well, I am still grateful for your help. Especially now that it's raining."

"I'll see about calling in some help for you once it lets up. That alright?"

"Uh huh. Ooh." She winced, and he moved to steady her as she lowered herself onto the cushions.

"Let's see that ankle," he said.

He might not be willing to trap her in the mountains with him as his mate, but he could help her. If it was broken, he'd carry her down the mountain himself once the storm passed. There was no way he'd risk a single thing happening to her.

Should've bought that quad, he cursed himself silently for not purchasing the all-terrain vehicle one of his contractors had suggested after construction was complete. But Keeton was a Shifter, he needed no help to move up and down the mountain. He just never counted on guests.

“Ouch.” She bit her lip as he undid her laces and tugged gently on her ankle high hiking sneakers.

The things were brand new, expensive, not the footwear he expected a seasoned hiker on the expert trail to wear. In his gut, he knew she was no experienced backpacker. Her skin was too fair, her equipment still had tags. This was one hell of a trek for her to take on her own.

What is she doing out here?

Marilena sucked in a sharp breath as he peeled off her sock to reveal her swollen ankle. It was turning a deep shade of purple, worrying him for the moment. His cat hissed. The creature did not like her injured at all and was ready to lay waste to the entire mountain for damaging his mate. Keeton hushed the silly beast.

Focusing instead on every nuance of movement the female made, he turned her foot slightly. Careful not to cause her further pain, he was sure to keep his movements steady and slow so he could assess the damage. As a soldier and mercenary, Keeton had experience with rendering first aid in the battlefield. And he'd never been more grateful for the experience than he was now.

"It's bruised, but it's not broken," he grunted.

"Oh, thank God!"

"Let me get you some ice."

He released his hold on her foot reluctantly. Practically had to force his fingers to open. Nodding slightly at her wide-eyed stare, he left the room. He hurried to the kitchen to grab some ice and then to the bathroom to get the first-aid kit. Catching his face in the mirror, he stopped and stared.

What the fucking fuck is wrong with me?

Too many things to count, for sure. He looked like a crazy person. For the first time in his life, his beard was over six inches long and his hair hung down to his shoulders in a shaggy mess. She must think him some kind of savage.

Fuck it.

She's better off without me, anyway.

Mine, snarled his cat, and he shook his head to quiet the sound of his inner beast.

He was not about to take advantage of an injured woman under his roof. Could not find a single reason why she would benefit from being with him. But maybe, just maybe, he could offer his animal a taste of being near her. Something to remember while he lived out the rest of his days deep in the mountain and away from society. Now that was a compromise, if ever he heard of one.

Keeton walked back to the living room to find Marilena had removed her other shoe and sock, her jacket and sweatshirt as well. She was unbuttoning her pants when he made some noise to alert her to his presence.

"Oh," she said, blushing a pretty shade of pink. "I wanted to get changed. I hope you don't mind. I sort of tore my jeans when I fell."

Keeton frowned and walked over to her, eyes intent on the two tears he somehow missed at both knees. He placed the first aid kit on the coffee table, then moved it back so he could get closer to her.

"Are you hurt anywhere else?"

"I don't think so, but these jeans are cutting into my waist. I have a pair of yoga pants in my backpack."

He grabbed the backpack and opened it, finding the black stretchy pants among her things. She sure had packed lightly, and not at all for the rough terrain. Definitely a novice. Again, he wondered what had made her climb up this way.

"If you could hand me that blanket..." She pointed to the crocheted afghan that sat on the armchair facing the fireplace, and he moved quickly to grab it.

He waited as she draped it over her waist, not telling her it was useless since not seeing her didn't stop him from scenting her, and it was her scent that drove him wild with need. He swallowed down his baser instincts and concentrated on helping her get comfortable.

"How can I help?"

"I think I can lift myself up if you wouldn't mind, tugging down my jeans?

I am so sorry to ask—"

"It's no trouble," he cut her off, waiting for her nod as he reached beneath the blanket to hold on to the denim at her waist.

He closed his eyes, praying for patience, and pulled the material carefully so as not to rip it clean off her. Fuck, he'd never had his control tested like that before. The sound of her pulse racing when he put his hands on her, the warm breath that tickled his ear lobes as he leaned in, and her honeyed scent that increased with his nearness.

She wanted him. Keeton cursed the Fates even as the knowledge made his chest, and other parts of him, swell with pride. It was the way of these things he'd often heard from other Shifters, even if he never experienced it himself. When the Fates matched up a pair, desire and need would often increase until they consummated the relationship and claimed one another.

Mating fever, or so it was termed between Shifters. He never realized a human could feel some of the effects as well.

Why else would this beautiful woman even consider him?

A whimper escaped her lips as she lifted onto her elbows and her one uninjured foot, and the leash he held on himself broke.

“Let me help,” he grunted and wrapped one arm around her waist, lifting her and tugging on the jeans the rest of the way past her hips.

"Sorry," she whispered.

"No need. Better now?" he asked as he slid the fabric carefully off her bruised ankle.

"Yes." She nodded and grabbed for her other pants.

"Wait. Let me make sure you aren't cut first." He waited for her assent, then lifted the blanket to her thighs.

Keeton frowned at the myriad of scrapes marring both her knees. He grabbed the first aid kit and cleaned them first with antiseptic wipes before applying antibiotic ointment and one large bandage on each.

"That should do it," he murmured.

"Thank you," she said, and he noted her breathing was easier.

Next, he helped her guide her legs

into her pants, but she stopped him before he could lift her again. He frowned, but did as she asked, turning around to give her some privacy.

"I'm so sorry for all this, and I can't thank you enough. Maybe I could write you a check?"

"You want to give me money for helping you?" he asked, a little shocked.

"Well, in my experience no one does anything for free—"

"I don't expect a reward for simply being decent."

"Most men I know would," she replied, and his beast came roaring to the surface once more.

"What men do that?"

"You'd be surprised."

"Men like who?"

“My ex-fiancé, for one. He’s a slimeball attorney.”

“A lawyer? No wonder,” he murmured.

“I know, right? My mom introduced us. I should’ve known better.”

“How did you get engaged to him?”

“I don’t know. He asked, and I was so surprised I said yes. I think I thought it was my only shot. Doesn’t matter now. It’s over. I, uh, caught him cheating.”

“Fuck. Look, I’m sorry, but it seems like his loss.”

“Yeah, right.” She snorted.

“I don’t know who you’ve been dealing with, but real men don’t take money from women just for helping them out. And they don’t cheat. Not ever.”

"I suppose you're right about that. Still, I feel like I should do something for all you've done." She shrugged, still blushing prettily.

"How about you rest here a minute? Let me fix you dinner, Marilena. Afterward, we can talk."

He handed her the ice pack before leaving the room. Keeton was sure it wasn't her intention to flirt, but that vulnerable look on her face as she asked him if there was something she could do for him damn near set him off. The bulge that was hopefully hidden behind his zipper and flannel was begging him to take her up on her offer, but he cursed himself ten times a fool.

She wasn't offering to sleep with him, for fuck's sake. Even if she was, he would not treat her that way. Besides, if Keeton allowed his desires to take over, there was no way he could guarantee he wouldn't claim the female.

Keeton was too fucked up to inflict himself on anyone permanently. Look at him. Like a fucking coward he ran to the mountains, hiding away from the entire world because some asshole discovered his secret and blackmailed him.

No. That was only half the reason. It was the disdain on the now dead man's face, the way his lips had curled, and eyes filled with hatred when he spat the one word guaranteed to pain any Shifter.

Animal.

He'd called Keeton an animal while demanding money to keep silent.

The Shifter secret was too big to let pride stand in his way. And it was not his alone to keep. So, he paid, then told his commanding officers about the situation, fully expecting to be kicked out of the unit. But he wasn't, and the other man had died in battle, not trusting Keeton to keep him alive cause he was just an animal.

No, he would not inflict himself on this beautiful woman. He couldn't live with the possibility of her rejecting him. He was man enough to admit that, even if only to himself. Not a chance. He would simply have to content himself with feeding her and tending her injuries.

It was all he had to offer the lovely human female.

CHAPTER FIVE

LENA LOOKED AROUND the sparsely decorated living room. The cabin was beautiful, but it felt so lonely, she thought, and a pang of sadness constricted her heart. There were no photographs or paintings, no color to break up the monotony of browns and tans.

Her gaze kept returning to the raging storm beyond the enormous floor to ceiling windows that faced the covered porch and the grassy field beyond. She heard Keeton moving about the kitchen. Quiet and self-assured, she couldn't imagine the mountain man needing anything at all, but still. She seemed to sense his loneliness, and it hurt her.

Silly, she knew, but she wanted to help somehow. Whatever had caused him to run away and hide from the world couldn't be that bad, she mused.

But what if it was?

Truthfully, she knew nothing about him. And yet, she had never felt so safe in her life. She must be really desperate for attention. Lena cursed herself for that thought. It was her mother's voice, not hers, that crept into her thoughts. Worming its way in whenever she was feeling peaceful or at ease.

"I hope you like stew." Keeton's voice penetrated the stark silence, and she jumped. "Shit, sorry. I didn't mean to startle you."

"No, no, please, you are fine. That was my fault, I got lost in my head." She shrugged and sat up, breathing in the aromatic stew he set on a bed tray over her legs.

"This smells wonderful!"

"Thanks." He shrugged, clearly embarrassed by her praise. "Nothing to it."

"I smell fresh rosemary and is that cinnamon?"

"Yeah, just a pinch."

He was really blushing now, but Lena was in her glory when discussing food. The first bite was heavenly. She could not stop herself from moaning aloud. The meat was tender.

"Is this rabbit?"

"Um, yeah. Is that okay?"

"Yes." She grinned. "I like rabbit. I imagine you do a lot of hunting up here."

"I do," he replied, and she smiled at him, hoping to ease some of his tension.

"It's delicious. So, is this like a weekend getaway?"

"The cabin? No, I live here."

"Like year round?"

"Yes," he said, placing his fork down beside his large bowl. "I built this place about two years ago and have been living here ever since."

"You never go into town?"

Keeton shook his head, and Lena's heart squeezed once more. Whatever ghosts filled his past and sent him running for the hills, she sure as hell hoped they would let up and leave him be. He was a good man. She could tell. Lena was sort of an expert after wasting so much of her time with the wrong kind of man.

"What's so funny?"

He seemed genuinely curious, and she realized then she'd snorted aloud at her own self-critique. There was something so open and honest about him, although she could tell he was keeping something to himself. It wasn't her business, she knew, even so, she was curious.

"I was just thinking that I wasted a lot of time on the wrong man, and for the first time in a long time I feel, well, un-anxious, if that's even a word."

Thunder crashed outside, the storm turning violent as she ate her dinner with the mysterious mountain man whose dark green eyes held such secrets she could hardly even imagine. Maybe she was wrong to trust him so blindly.

But what choice did Lena really have?

"I think it's good that you feel at ease, Marilena," he said after a brief pause.

She could tell she'd pleased him with her statement, though she had no actual idea why. What should he care for her comfort, or discomfort for that matter? And yet, this stranger had showed her more kindness since she'd met him than Cary had in all of their months of living together and being engaged to be married.

"It's been a while since I've felt that. My mother is always telling me how foolish I am and constantly correcting me. She doesn't necessarily approve of my life choices."

"Why is that?"

"Well, for one thing, I'm overweight and had to be unforgivably obvious about it by going into the food industry. You see, I run a catering business, and I am not sure what she finds worse, that her fat daughter likes food or that she's made it her life's work."

"Apologies to your mother, but she doesn't know what the hell she's talking about," he replied in a firm tone that made her heart skip a beat.

"Well, you hardly know me." She shrugged.

"I know we don't really know each other, Marilena, but it doesn't take a lifetime for me to look at you to see you're beautiful."

"Ha, now you're being nice," she said, embarrassed now that she brought up her looks.

"Even if I was, it's true," he returned earnestly. "From what I can see, you look exactly how a woman should. The fact you are passionate about your work only makes you more genuine, and damn lucky too. Few people can say that."

"I guess that's true. I mean, my mother has never worked a day in her life, so I don't expect her to understand how I feel when I am on a job. I mean the feeling I get when I am catering a wedding or anniversary party, something that brings people together to celebrate, is simply unparalleled. My food helps those families enjoy themselves. Food brings people together, and I am proud of my work."

"See, right there." He pointed with his fork. "I'm looking at you, watching you talk about your work, and you are radiant."

"Oh, um, thanks." She licked her lips, a bit shy of his praise.

"I'm sorry if I overstepped," he blurted. Again, she'd swear he sounded sincere. "I think anyone who makes you feel uncomfortable or like doubting yourself isn't worth your time. You shouldn't even consider them."

"You know, you are really easy to talk to for a giant mountain man."

"Um. Are you finished?" he asked abruptly.

Lena nodded. Cheeks flushed, she wiped her mouth on the napkin and replaced it on the tray. Watching him walk away, tray and empty bowls in hand proved more interesting than the storm, despite the brilliant flashes of lightning that illuminated the sky.

OMG, I can't believe I said that.

She scolded herself silently. Lena

really had a way of sticking her foot in her mouth time and again.

Brilliant.

Truly.

Full and no longer in pain, she lay back and sighed. It was foolish, silly, and a little naïve on her part. Totally unreal that she felt so perfectly peaceful with the enormous stranger, and yet, as her eyelids grew heavy, she realized quite unsurprisingly that she trusted Keeton Grey.

Trusted him to keep her safe and dry from the storm outside, but, a little nagging voice whispered inside her sleepy head, who would keep her safe from the storm of emotions threatening to burst free inside her?

CHAPTER SIX

KEETON RETURNED TO the living room to find the object of his growing affection sleeping soundly on his sofa. Much as he'd like to leave her be, the couch was no place for a lady to slumber.

He steadied himself. Touching her was like holding a live wire, asleep or not. Every single inch of him seemed attuned to her body. He wanted to make her feel good, to satisfy her every desire and craving, and yet, it was not his place. She was not his. He would not claim her.

He'd staked out his life in the Panther Mountains long before he'd ever stumbled upon the gorgeous creature, and there he would stay, long after she'd gone. Back to the world where she belonged. But while she was there, he could at least make her comfortable. He owed her that.

Keeton leaned down, scooping her up gently. She snuggled closer into his chest, sighing contentedly. The soft sounds stroked his cat and his ego. Both beast and man proud that she sought him out, even in sleep, for comfort.

We could give her more than just comfort.

We could bring her to such heights, show her pleasure she's never experienced.

No. He shut down that train of thought. Keeton was far more interested in her well being than in his carnal desires. The beautiful Marilena deserved more than he could deliver in the one night she would share a roof with him. It was better this way.

All night long, Keeton paced the cabin. He was restless, emotions a mess. She would be gone soon, and he could get back to his secluded lifestyle.

He brewed some coffee and turned

on the small radio he used to keep up with the world whenever he felt too isolated. But the news was not good.

That night had brought down part of the mountain in a mudslide the likes of which he'd never encountered. The pass was unreachable until further notice. Fuck, he hadn't counted on that complication. And what was worse, the thunderstorms currently raging were soon to become ice and possible blizzard conditions.

It seemed an unseasonably cold front was hitting the Garden State, and the Panther Mountains were going to see the worst of it. Fuck. He should have gone out in the rain last night and called a rescue team to come get her. What was he going to do now? Stuck inside with her for days was going to be a veritable nightmare.

He banged on the counter and sucked in a breath. He couldn't do this. Couldn't be trapped inside with her for the unforeseeable future. It was impossible. Keeton just wasn't sure he could control himself, much less his beast.

"Is everything okay?"

Fuck. When had she come into the room? He turned around to face her, unprepared for the concern marring her otherwise soft features. Cursing himself a fool, he walked over to her and held out the chair.

"What are you doing out of bed?"

"How I got in bed is the real question," she said with renewed laughter that lightened his heart.

"I didn't want you to get a cramp on the couch," he murmured as she eased into the chair.

Keeton grabbed a stepstool and a few clean kitchen towels and propped her injured foot on top. Lena tucked her hair behind her ears, looking anywhere but at him. At first, he was confused, then he realized he was shirtless.

She likes my body, he thought with pride, *and something else* swelling inside him.

"Coffee?"

"Yes, please."

He grabbed a mug and poured her some, offering her the can of evaporated milk he'd recently opened. He preferred it to powdered creamer. Though he had fresh supplies brought in every few months, it had been a while between deliveries.

"Thanks," she replied shyly. "So, any news about getting someone up here to get me out of your hair?"

"Oh, um, actually, I was just listening to the radio. It seems the storm brought down some of the mountain. The path where I usually get reception is unreachable. I mean, I could try—"

"No! I mean, no, please. I don't want you getting hurt. But, well, do you mind? Me having to stay another day?"

"Truth is, Lena, you might be stuck here for more than a day. We're getting a cold front too. They are predicting snow and sleet. A couple of feet of it by tomorrow night."

"What? I mean, I wasn't even wearing a jacket last week!"

"I know. It's global warming. Too much stress on our planet is wreaking havoc with weather patterns. I promise, I'll keep you safe," he said, meaning to assure her.

"I know that, but I feel so bad intruding—"

"Don't give it another thought. It's the least I can do."

"I swear, I've never met a man like you. Look, I am going to take you up on your offer because I have no choice really," she said and laughed a little. "I will be undoubtedly cutting into your supplies, so I insist you take me up on my offer to pay you."

"I won't take money from you," he

growled, cutting off the sound so as not to frighten her.

He could not help it, though. His cat was incensed that she would try to pay him. It was his honor and privilege to care for her.

Mine.

Mate.

Shhh.

He quieted the angry cat and refocused his attention on her. Not hard to do since she was the only damn thing he'd been thinking about for the last eighteen hours.

Grrr.

"Okay, fine. No money. But I insist on cooking today. Deal?"

He waited a beat. Not completely happy with her decision to work off her imaginary debt to him, but Keeton tried to see it from her perspective. She was independent, proud, and totally adorable. He had no wish to take any of that away from her, so he agreed.

"Fine, but I get to assist you."

"Okay."

Surprised by her ready acquiescence, he looked up and froze like a deer in headlights. Marilena was smiling at him, and it was like the sun peeking through the clouds after weeks of nothing but rain. He swallowed down his desire, trying for calm when he felt anything but.

Her iridescent eyes glittered at him from across the table. A gorgeous combination of rusty bronze and moss green, she blinked them slowly behind long, thick eyelashes. His heart squeezed in response at their otherworldly beauty.

Keeton had never seen a woman with her coloring. Golds and greens like some Celtic goddess, though her name screamed her Italian heritage. Must have been the Vikings, he mused.

"What are you thinking about that has you grinning so?"

"Nothing," he replied.

"Come on. Tell me. I love a good story with my coffee."

"Well, I was just wondering about you."

"What about me?"

"Your family is Italian, right?"

"Yes," she answered, seemingly pleased with his interest. "I have Italian blood on both sides of my family. Though my mother is third or fourth generation American, my father was born in Italy."

"Really?"

"Yes. I didn't know him well, though," she answered, looking down at her mug.

"Must be the Vikings," he said, and rapped his knuckles on the table.

"Beg your pardon?"

"Your eyes and hair. Must be the Vikings."

"I don't get it." She laughed, clearly game for his explanation, and damn, but he was charmed.

Loved seeing that smile on her face, and the good humor glittering in her eyes. He wanted to make her smile again and again for as long as he was able.

Forever.

His Mountain Lion seemed to think that was a possibility, but Keeton refused to enter that dream.

That way lies madness.

She was beautiful and vibrant. He could not bear to think of her wasting away on a mountain just to be with him. It was unthinkable to even ask it.

"Well? What Vikings?" she asked, interrupting his inner turmoil.

"Oh," he said, remembering where he'd left off. "There was a guy from New York in my first special ops unit—"

"You were in the military?"

Keeton stilled.

Shit.

He hadn't meant to reveal anything

about himself to her. But she was just so easy to talk to. How could he harbor secrets from his fated mate? Impossible. Resigned, he nodded and continued his tale.

"Yeah. Anyway, he was almost as tall as me, with this crazy white-blond hair and bright blue eyes. All the guys ribbed him about not really being Italian. Finally, one night we were waiting for orders to move forward on an enemy encampment. Dangerous territory. There were these really evil militant fuckers trying to take over the government of a small nation. They were heavily armed and had these animal-like pens filled with civilians surrounding their enclosure for protection against us—"

"That's despicable," she said, and her outrage on his behalf did something inside of him. He looked at her long and hard before continuing his story.

"Yeah. It was. So, we were waiting in the sweltering heat of this jungle, the air was so thick it was like my aunt's giblet gravy on Thanksgiving. Everyone was tense, agitated with all the waiting. Then New York, that's what we called him, well, he turned all seriousness waving his hands for everyone to look at him. 'I got it,' he said, 'I know why I'm so tall and blond that none of you bozos believe I'm Italian. It was those damn Vikings!' Hell, we all laughed so hard our commanding officer wrote rips for all of us. But it was good. We relaxed, waited for our orders, and got the job done without one civilian casualty."

"Wow," she said, leaning on the table.

"Shit. I'm sorry if I made you uncomfortable—" Keeton apologized, not knowing why he felt the need to tell that damn story to begin with.

"What was his name?"

"Who?"

"New York."

"Oh. His name was Rafael DiMare."

"Did he make it home?"

"Yeah. He did."

"And so did you."

"Yes," he replied cautiously, watching to see her next move.

Marilena stood up, not looking at him. Her wavy hair was a tangle down her back and her clothes were wrinkled from sleep, but he swore he'd never seen a woman more beautiful. She put her half-filled mug down on the table and moved until she was directly in front of him. Then, with no warning or sign, she opened her arms and drew him to her body, wrapping Keeton up in her warmth.

She just stood there and held him. Not speaking or moving for a good long while until his arms came up of their own volition and he returned the embrace. What started as a gesture meant to comfort, after some minutes became something else. Keeton tightened his arms, and raised his head.

Even from his position sitting down on a kitchen chair, he was just a smidge shorter than her. She couldn't be more than five-five, but Marilena was a treasure, regardless of height. He brushed her hair back from her face, running his fingers along her neck and cheeks until he held her face in his hands.

"Marilena," he gasped her name before crushing his lips to hers.

The fact she went willingly into the kiss was a shock to his system. But the kiss itself, well, that was the genuine surprise. The moment their lips touched, it was like a torrent of emotion released, threatening to drown him in the mad rush of desire, destiny, and deliciousness.

He stood, lifting her up in his embrace so she retained her height over him. Keeton backed them up until they hit the kitchen wall, careful to cradle her head with his hands so as not to injure. Never that.

Need grappled with desire until he didn't know which emotion was the fore. But his own turbulent feelings were nothing compared to hers. Nothing else mattered since the moment he kissed her. Nothing else ever would. Marilena was the single most important thing in his world. He could admit that now. Even if he couldn't keep her.

Mine.

CHAPTER SEVEN

HOLY SHIT.

Marilena never had much luck with men. Even with Cary, their bedroom antics were less than extraordinary. Significantly less.

But kissing this man, this virtual stranger, was like the culmination of every single fantasy she had indulged in since she fell in love with dramatic gothic heroes like Heathcliff and Edward Fairfax Rochester back in high school. Of course, in her opinion, Keeton Grey was not nearly as flawed as the two fictional characters. Besides, he was real. A living, breathing man. And at that very moment, he was kissing her better than anyone ever had.

Lena moaned as she sucked on his tongue, drinking in his unique flavors, and committing them to memory.

Maybe this was it?

Her destiny?

At worst, it was the only time she'd ever come close to having a truly remarkable sexual experience. Even if it was on top of a mountain with a strange, yet gorgeous, mystery man.

"Fuck, Lena, you taste like rosewater and honey," he whispered, kissing her lips like she was something precious.

She'd never been compared to something so delicate and lovely before. She was used to something more like 'your face is pretty, too bad you're so chubby' type compliments from men. Even Cary. The asshole.

But all thoughts of other men, even her ex-fiancé, left her brain when he started touching her. Gently, respectfully, and oh-so-tenderly, Keeton found her breast beneath the rumpled cotton tee shirt she slept in. His palm swallowed even her sizeable assets, the heated skin brushing against her hardened nub sent a flood of desire coursing through her veins and culminating between her legs.

“Want you,” he growled, nipping the sensitive skin at her neck.

“Yes,” she replied, nodding vigorously. “Oh, yes.”

His emerald eyes caught hers, and he seemed to be weighing the verity of her statement. She let him stare. Hell, she encouraged it, wanting him to see the stark desire in her eyes. She knew it must be there, plain as the nose on her face, cause in all her thirty years on this planet, she had never felt anything close to what she felt for him.

This was more than desire. This was a bone-deep hunger. An ache that only Keeton Grey could satisfy. She did not know how she knew it, but the truth of that statement made her blood sing.

"I want you too, Keeton."

The statement spurred him on like nothing else seemed to. He cupped her ass in his large, powerful hands and carried her back to the room where she woke up that morning. He placed her gently on the covers she'd rearranged like any good guest just minutes ago.

Heat, passion, desire. Take your pick. They all motivated her as clothes were removed, some torn in their haste to get each other naked. Usually shy, Lena felt emboldened by the way he looked at her. She arched her back, giving him a better view, and he hissed in return like a scalded cat.

The sound was deeper, though, animalistic. But she was not frightened.

In fact, she reveled in his loss of the ability to speak. It made her feel powerful, beautiful, and wanted. Something she had not felt in an awfully long time, if ever.

"Keeton," she moaned his name, propelling the gorgeous mountain man into action.

"Beautiful," he growled the word, leaning over her to rain kisses on her face and chest.

Keeton ran his hands down her body, from her neck, between the valley of her breasts, over her soft belly, straight to her needy core. He left no part of her untouched as he explored all of Marilena's secrets. A thousand and one emotions rolled through her, the least of which not being pure pleasure.

Never had she felt like so much joy from a man's embrace. Keeton's hands were positively magic. She was insatiable for his touch. Wanted him anywhere, everywhere, as long as he never stopped.

"Please," she whimpered as he trailed hot, open-mouthed kisses along her skin.

Her nipples tightened, breasts swelled, and pussy dripped with need. As if he read her mind, he closed his lips over one plump mound while his fingers parted her slick sex lips. She moaned aloud, begging him without words to continue the sensual assault that had her arching into his touch, mindless with need.

"Taste so good," he growled, tugging

her nipple between his teeth. "I want more. Want it all."

He licked his way down her body, whispering words of praise and appreciation for her plus-size frame. Lena watched him through heavy-lidded eyes as he settled between her thighs, using his wide shoulders to spread her legs even further.

She expected him to get down to it, but Keeton was not a man to be rushed. Biting her lip, she held her breath as he simply stared at her sex. No one had ever done that before. But he was doing it. Just looking at her needy little sex, plump and wet, waiting for him to stake his claim.

"Keeton," she whimpered his name.

Her cheeks heated, and she felt her

blush spread, covering her body in a deep shade of pink. But he still did not move. His rapt stare nearly undid her. The man was all intensity, but she was a woman unused to such attention. She didn't know how to react or what to do. Then she didn't have to worry because he did it for her.

"Beautiful," he murmured, and lowered his head, gifting her with one hot, open-mouthed kiss right on her pussy.

Lena saw stars. She moaned aloud, head falling back as he kissed and kissed *and kissed* her, long and good. She gripped the bedding in her fists, trying to move her hips, but he pinned her down with his enormous hands while he feasted on her.

Holy fuck.

The man was an animal. And she meant that in the best possible way. Her clit throbbed as his tongue sought her core. And just like before, he read her mind, using his thumb to strum the needy little nubbin while he stroked along her channel.

"Keeton," she moaned.

Then switched places. He lapped at her pussy like a kitty licking cream from a bowl. Strumming her clit with his rough-sided tongue while plunging his fingers deep into her channel. Green eyes met hers as she watched him devouring her, and damn, she had never seen a man so sexy or hungry in her life.

Finally, he let go of her hips, allowing

her to rock against him, driving toward a fulfillment only he could deliver. She had no doubt Keeton Grey was going to rock her world. In fact, she was willing to bet everything on it. Then it was happening. That slowly growing pleasure he delivered so expertly exploded into a myriad of sensations, sending Lena shooting over the edge like a star through the sky.

"Mine," he growled.

She was in no condition to deny the caveman like declaration. In fact, deep down, she sorta wished he really meant it. Lena tried to catch her breath, but she'd have better luck trying to catch a fish with her bare hands. Her mountain man was a veritable sex god.

Keeton lapped at her pussy one last

time before crawling up her body. She rose up, kissing his lips while he spread her legs with his hands and placed the head of his magnificent cock at her slick entrance.

"You sure you want—" he said, his voice barely recognizable, and that was a turn on in itself.

"Yes," she responded before he'd even finished his question.

Overwhelmed with emotion, she flexed her hips, taking him deep inside her body. For the first time in her entire life, Marilena felt whole. His glorious cock filled her completely. Every miraculous inch stroked along her inner walls, touching that secret place no other man had ever reached.

She'd never been particularly lusty or

wanton, but he made her want things she'd never even dreamed of. Keeton cradled her face in his massive hands, making her feel small and cherished. He kissed her lips tenderly, prolonging the sweet contact up until he started to move.

Then all bets were off. Lena bucked wildly, scratching his back like a hellion. She screamed his name, clawed his skin, and yes, she even bit him when he made her come for the third time in a row. All the while he encouraged her, said the most deliciously naughty things, and fuck, she thought she might have even fallen in love with him just then.

He switched positions, lying flat on his back with Lena astride. At first, she faltered, uncertain of her ability to take him that way.

"You can take me, baby," he whispered, reading her mind once more. "That's it. Move, just like that. So fucking good."

He ran his hands up her sides and back down over her breasts. Keeton cupped the mounds as if testing their weight. Then he squeezed, adding just enough force to his touch, plucking her nipples while she rotated her hips, grinding down on his enormous shaft. Head tossed back, Lena rode him as if she were born to do it.

To do him, she thought with a naughty grin.

Sex had always been embarrassing for her, and downright unfulfilling. But with him, Lena felt so much more than she'd ever thought possible. His hands clutched her hips, and he took over. Lifting and slamming her back down on his dick. Faster, harder, and so deep, she trembled from head to foot with the power of his ministrations. Every thrust brought her that much closer to the edge.

Each swipe of his tongue across her skin, his lips on her collarbone, those fingers digging into her ass pushed her one inch closer to that pinnacle of ecstasy she saw destined for her in his evergreen gaze. Like it was his own personal promise to fuck her into oblivion. Lena was more than game, she demanded it. Wanted that paradise she saw in his eyes for herself. Wanted him to go there with her.

"Come for me, Lena, do it, now," he commanded.

She felt her sex squeezing him tightly. It was as if her body could not bear to disobey his wishes. Then she was coming, hard and fast, and somehow everlasting. Every nerve was pulsing with raw, unadulterated passion, and still he moved. Flexing his hips, Keeton ground her down hard onto his shaft.

Someone screamed, a raw, guttural noise that shook the entire cabin. Could have been either of them, or maybe it was both of them. Lena could not think, she could only feel. And right then, what she felt was him inside every single cell.

It seemed like hours later before she

could even breathe, but it was probably only minutes.

Either way, what was time?

Keeton lifted her off him, both moaning at the sudden loss, then he cradled her close. Tucking her into his side, he held her like that until they both nodded off. For the first time in her life, Marilena drifted into a dreamless sleep born of utter exhaustion and satisfaction.

She didn't want to think about what would happen when they both woke up. She just wanted to revel in the unparalleled connection she'd just shared.

"Mine," she thought she heard him whisper.

If only I were yours.

CHAPTER EIGHT

MINE.

Mine.

MINE!

What the fuck was he doing?

Keeton could hardly think coherently. Fuck that. He didn't want to think. He just wanted to feel. It was extraordinary. Momentous. A fucking epiphany. Whatever you wanted to call it, it was the best damn sex of his life.

Loving on Marilena with everything in him was second to breathing. He did not have to fake it or work at it, nor was he just going through the motions to sate a biological urge.

He knew the second she pressed her soft body to his that he wouldn't be able to hold on to his control. Desire for her just came naturally. But unlike any other female he'd been with, her pleasure came first. Her needs were paramount to his, and he made damn well sure she'd felt good the whole time.

Fucking hell.

He could not believe that just happened. He'd just made love to the woman the universe had made for him and him alone. Keeton had long since given up on the idea that he had a fated mate out there. Meeting her had proved him wrong. But loving her, well, that had been something else entirely.

She was so sweet, so generous. A wildcat with unbridled passion only tendered by her own willingness to give as generously as she got. Her responsiveness to his touch was awesome. Like really awesome, not the Bill & Ted version of the word.

Every whimper and moan, the sound of her silken skin sliding against his, her pants and cries were symphonic. She tasted like fresh honey and rose petals. Sort of like this pistachio rose petal covered *Turkish Delight* he'd once had overseas, only better. So much better.

His Mountain Lion scratched and chuffed deep inside him. The animal was thrilled he'd pleased their mate, but he was pissed as hell that Keeton had not claimed her. A Mountain Lion Shifter claimed his fated mate with a *mating bite.*

He'd managed to stop himself before he could bind her to him for eternity.

A mistake?

Maybe.

But he needed to speak with her before doing such a thing. He couldn't just kidnap her and force her to live in the mountains with him.

Follow her then. Live where she lives. His Lion urged, but Keeton shook his head.

No.

My home is here.

It was a dilemma. One he was not sure how to handle. For now, he'd simply hold her. Her steady breaths told him she was sleeping. He growled softly, pressing a kiss to her forehead, and wrapping her loosely in his arms. He loved the fact she was in his bed. With any luck, the mattress would carry her scent for weeks to come after she'd gone.

His beast snarled at the thought. But it did not matter what his animal thought. The woman was human. She would not be staying. There was an entire world out there for her to see. A world Keeton was no longer a part of.

He just couldn't be.

What did the world hold for him anymore?

More lies and betrayal?

Distrust?

He'd almost let his biggest secret fall into the wrong hands. Fuck that. He had let it fall into the wrong hands, and it had cost him. Half a million dollars, and the other man, *his blackmailer*, well, it had cost him his life.

But it was all Keeton's fault. Had he been in control of his shift, none of that would have happened. He was better off alone, isolated from the rest of humanity.

But Lena?

Nah.

She was meant for the sunshine.

He supposed he should just take the gift he was given and enjoy it. No matter how fleeting.

***

A few hours later…

"This is ridiculously good!" Lena moaned her pleasure while taking a bite of his spaghetti carbonara.

"The trick, of course, is to eat it right away." He scooted in close behind her and opened his mouth for a bite of the delicious pasta dish he'd learned how to cook when he'd been stationed in Naples.

"Mmm hmm," she agreed, nodding at him with her mouth full of deliciousness.

"How do you have fresh eggs?"

"I freeze them in single serve packets. Just have to throw them in the fridge to thaw out overnight and use them like you usually would."

"Really? I did not know that. And this parsley? It tastes too fresh to be frozen."

"I have a mini greenhouse just behind the kitchen. I'll show you later if you like."

"I'd love that."

"Happy to oblige, Chef Sorelli." Keeton loved making her blush when he used her professional title. So far, he hadn't let her do much with her ankle still swollen and bruised. Besides, he liked her this way. Half-dressed and sitting between his spread legs on the carpet in front of the fireplace. She was wearing his shirt and nothing underneath, but he'd never seen any woman look better than she did.

"This is good, but I make a *Mahalabia* that'll knock your socks off," she said, biting her lower lip, tempting him to kiss the hurt she inflicted there.

"What's that?"

"It's a type of Middle Eastern pudding made with milk and special rose and orange blossom waters, garnished with dried rose petals and crushed pistachios. I add a drizzle of organic lavender honey to mine."

"Sounds delicious," he growled.

Fuck.

His Mountain Lion was pushing for dominance. Every second he spent with her, he risked losing more of himself, but it was worth it. She was incredible. Funny, smart, so beautiful it hurt to look at her. Not to mention her generosity.

"I'd like to make you some."

"I'd like that too, but there is something I'd like even better."

"Oh, yeah?" Her hazel eyes glittered like green gold in the light from the fireplace, and Keeton forgot how to breathe for a moment.

"Yessss," he hissed the word. It seemed his inner feline was determined to make an appearance, and yet, he wasn't sure that was a good idea at all.

Hadn't he already decided not to keep her?

"Keeton," she murmured, turning around in his arms, and crashing her lips to his.

Her kisses were so warm and enthusiastic. Like sunshine and rollercoaster rides. She was beautifully uninhibited. Sweet and innocent. Way too good for him.

He should put a stop to this. Really, he should. And he would. In another minute, or ten. But he was helpless to push her away when she lifted her legs over his thighs, pressing her naked heat to his boxer clad sex, purring like a kitten deep in her throat while her tongue teased his in a wicked game of tag.

“Lena,” he growled, holding her still and taking what he wanted.

Two moves was all it would take, then he’d be buried to the hilt in sweet erotic bliss. She seemed to know that too. Before he could decide just what he was going to do, Lena had him in the palm of her hand. Literally.

She stroked his cock from root to tip, smearing the pearl of precum that had leaked from his slit around the mushroomed head. All the while she kissed him, lavishing attention on his mouth with her clever lips and tongue. Kissing her was more addictive than any narcotic, he was positive.

Better than chocolate.

Even the good kind.

"Fuck, baby, that feels so good."

Keeton had no qualms about letting her take charge. Hell, he was primed and ready for anything she wanted to do. Groaning aloud, he sure as fuck went cross-eyed when she lifted her sweet ass off the floor, positioning his cock right at her sopping entrance.

"You feel good too," she said, sinking down onto his shaft, swallowing every one of his eleven and a half inches, but slowly.

So fucking slow, Keeton nearly came right then and there.

"I can't," he growled when she did it again, lifting herself high on her knees, until he almost slipped free, then sliding down again, taking him all the way deep inside her most secret treasure.

"You can," she moaned. "You feel so good, Keeton. Your cock feels so good inside me."

Up and down.

Slow withdraw, equally slow slide

back down.

Fucking hell.

This was sweet torture. But it was almost too much. Head thrown back, she looked like a goddess, pumping him with her sweat-slickened body. All curves and valleys, hidden dips, and tempting little hills. She was a masterpiece. A real flesh and blood woman, more beautiful than any he'd ever known.

A rainbow of colors from her hazel eyes to her russet hair, creamy skin, dusky pink lips, and inky black lashes. He would never have his fill of her. Not today, tomorrow, or a hundred years from then.

Of course, she knew nothing about Shifters or fated mates. And he wasn't gonna tell her.

Mine.

No.

Yessssss.

Fuck.

He was gonna come. But no way was he going without her. Keeton flipped their positions. Rising up on his knees with Lena flat on her back, he lifted her thighs up over his shoulders and proceeded to fuck her long and hard.

"Oh, God!"

"Not God. Keeton," he growled.

He wanted her to say his name. Needed to hear it on her lips. Wanted to be the only man, the only person she called out to in passion. His cat demanded it, as a matter of fact.

Pumping his hips, he lowered one

hand and strummed her exposed clit. Kneading the swollen nubbin until he felt quivers from her pussy flutter around his cock, squeezing him like a vise.

"Keeton. Keeton. KEETON!"

"That's right," he grunted, pumping once, twice more, and filling her with his seed.

If he would not claim her, at least she could wear his scent. That would placate the beast inside him. For a little while anyway.

A sudden pounding on the doorway had Keeton snarling angrily. He cut off the sound, aware of Lena's wide-eyed stare even as he helped her sit up and righted her shirt.

"Anyone home?"

He really wanted to say no. But he knew that fucking voice. Figured the asshole had come to check on him and gotten caught in the blizzard outside.

Frigging Bears.

But Niels Orson was more than just a Bear Shifter pain in Keeton's ass. He was one of his closest friends. He and Silas McKennon had formed a bond during training when they'd first joined the military.

Though they'd been separated into different units, they'd still kept in touch through the years. All three had been picked by certain undisclosed black ops commanders who had taken it upon themselves to create specialized task forces that eventually turned into private military missions.

Before the three men knew it, they were working for the personal armies of one or more governments. All wars were hopeless. One side forever doomed to failure. But it was the countless deaths Keeton had a hard time with. Niels and Silas shared that sorrow. His blood brothers carried that same weight heavy on their hearts.

Yes, they all dealt with it in their own way. Silas had returned to his father's multi-million dollar corporation in the big city, burying his head in paperwork and legalities. Niels was a drifter, living off his sizeable earnings. He wandered from place to place, never really settling in, or trying to, for that matter.

Niels hid behind his constant stranger's smile in every new town or village he happened upon. No roots, no permanence. He'd been to visit Keeton a few times since he had settled in the Panther Mountains. So, this little visit was not at all unusual.

Keeton, Silas, and Niels were a trio of broken men. Bound by their inability to find the peace of mind all soldiers sought after battle. The three of them once joked about how fucked they were for life. Only now, with Marilena currently dressing in his bedroom, Keeton wasn't so sure if that held true.

Not for him.

Not anymore.

"Keeton? What the fuck, brother? I know you're there. Open up. I'm freezing my dick off out here!"

"You have a brother?" Lena asked,

jostling him into action.

“Uh, sort of. Come on, let me help you inside so you can get dressed, sweet.” He lifted her in his arms, ignoring her shocked gasp and deposited her in the bedroom with speed he’d have a hell of a time explaining later. She was a human, after all.

Before he closed the door behind him, he grabbed a pair of sweats from his laundry basket and shrugged them on. Then he went to the front door, where Niels waited.

“Sup bro?” The man walked in and inhaled, a look of shock and mischief crossing his face before he turned back to Keeton. “Who’s the meat? She into doing multiples?”

Keeton snarled angrily. He had one

claw-tipped hand wrapped around his blood brother's throat in less time than it took to respond verbally. Rage and fury coursed through his veins at the casual insult the idiot hurled about his mate. A Shifter should know better.

"Fuck!" he gasped, trying without success to remove Keeton's hand from his throat. "Okay, okay! Fuck, I'm sorry, man!"

"Do not speak about her that way. Don't even look at her. Understand?"

"Fuck, yes. Let me down, you fucking lunatic!"

His Mountain Lion was not appeased by Niels' groveling. He squeezed just a fraction tighter, snarling angrily. Keeton felt fur sprout from his arms and knew even then his face was sharpening with his animal's fury. Holding a half-shift was tough as fuck, but he managed.

He snapped his teeth, hissing at Niels, who averted his gaze angrily. The Bear did not wish to challenge his friend. Keeton reined in his beast. Then he loosened his hold and dropped Niels on the floor right in the pile of melting slush the man had trekked inside.

Keeton ran a hand through his wild mane of hair and turned to the hall closet for a towel. He hurled it at the fucker. Hands on his hips, he tried to regulate his breathing, but the beast still wanted to rage at Niels for what he'd said about Lena.

Mine.

He closed his eyes and counted to ten. It seemed stupid, but it had worked for him before, Just the simplicity of the numbers, of reciting something he knew with ease, helped him push the animal back down.

"Keeton, bro. I think your lady has a question," Niels eyebrows disappeared into his hairline as the man gestured behind where Keeton stood.

Oh fuck.

He froze. His supernaturally enhanced hearing strained to hear her.

Why the fuck hadn't he sensed her?

He wanted to curse, but waited, listening instead to the unsteady rhythm of her heartbeat.

"Uh, Keeton?" Her husky voice sounded weak, far away.

"Lena, I can explain—"

"Okay, but do you think you could

catch me first?"

Niels was there before him, catching his mate before she hit the ground in a dead faint. He snarled angrily, but the man just shrugged, his arms full of Keeton's sweet mate.

"Dude? The fuck? You want me to drop her?"

"No! Just give her here," he growled, and took the precious bundle into his arms.

She weighed nothing at all. So soft and warm. His beautiful Marilena snuggled close to his bare chest, unconsciously seeking him out for comfort. He brought her back to the bedroom and laid her down on the mattress. He pulled the blanket up and over her still form, caressing her face tenderly when he felt Niels standing in the doorway.

He turned back to the man, his jaw clenched with worry. Keeton wiped his hands over his face and hair. He did not know what the fuck he was going to do now. She'd seen him in his half-shift. This was bad. Really bad.

"So, you found your mate?" Niels asked, handing him a short glass of the fifty-year-old Scotch he kept on a cart in the living room.

"Yeah, I guess I did." Keeton drained it in one shot.

Shifters didn't really get drunk. In order to feel the effects of drugs or alcohol, they either had to be magically enhanced or they had to be taken in massive quantities and quickly too.

"You didn't tell her about yourself?" Niels asked, his disbelief clear.

"I couldn't. Not yet. I mean, fuck, Niels. I live in the mountains. She's human. I don't know if this can work."

"But she is your mate? Don't you know it's a one in a million chance? Only the luckiest Shifters find their fated mates, Keeton. You have to give this a try."

"Why? Being my fated mate is no guarantee she will accept me for who I am, what I am. It's no guarantee I can make her happy. How can I all the way up here? You think a woman like that wants to live in the woods with a fucking hermit like me?"

"Dude, you have to give it a chance—"

"No! Whether she rejects me now or

later, it will happen. She has to go back. Her life is with people, mine is here. I just hope she can keep our damn secret—"

"Of course, I can." Lena's voice was huskier than before, thick with unshed tears he saw gleaming in her eyes when he turned to face her.

She had her arms wrapped around her waist and looked so fucking small and hurt, he wanted to kick his own ass for being an inconsiderate prick. He took one step toward her, but she backed up, and the movement cut through him like a knife.

"Lena, I—"

"I am so sorry I intruded on your privacy, Mr. Grey. I promise to leave as soon as the weather stops." She turned around and ran back to the bedroom, closing the door behind her.

It was no good. He heard her sobs, and his hurt only grew. He turned to see Niels growling at him and knew the man couldn't help it. It was in their nature to protect those weaker than them, especially females. Hell, his own Mountain Lion was doing one hell of a job clawing at him on the inside.

He'd fucked up.

Badly.

CHAPTER NINE

MARILENA, YOU FOOL.

How could you fall in love with him?

Lena sniffed and wiped her face. She'd retreated to Keeton's bedroom after she overheard him speaking to his friend.

What else could she do?

Okay. So he'd been keeping secrets. A big furry one apparently. A hysterical laugh escaped her lips, and she covered her mouth with both hands.

Was that really real?

The thing she saw.

Lena wasn't exactly prone to flights of fancy. She certainly never hallucinated before. But sure as she'd just spent the day wrapped around that gorgeous mountain man, she'd seen fur, claws, and fangs sprout from his body only minutes ago.

"You're a big girl, Lena. You can face this," she reasoned, forcing herself to walk to the mirror.

She looked a mess. Her hair was sleep tousled, face red and puffy from crying, and she still wore only his shirt.

There was a door to the bathroom inside his bedroom, and she decided she was going to have to prepare herself for the upcoming conversation. Best way to do that was with a shower.

Her knapsack was on the floor, so she had some of her things at least. Though pickings were slim when it came to clothing choices. She would simply have to make do. Her ankle was still bruised, but the swelling had gone down. Still, she needed to move slow and steady so as not to injure herself any farther.

She stepped into the warm spray of water and bathed her skin with a bar of almond-scented oatmeal soap that reminded her of his scent. Next, she washed her hair, taking the time to condition it too. It would make it easier to brush that way.

Afterward, she dressed in her last remaining clean pair of stretch pants, borrowing one of his thick thermal tops from his closet and a pair of long socks. Lena braided her hair, calming herself with the work of separating it into sections first, then winding the long strands around each other methodically.

Once finished, she looked at herself in the mirror. Lena hadn't bothered to bring any makeup with her. Even if she had, she couldn't put it on after crying with her eyes red and puffy. Besides, nothing in her cosmetics bag was going to cover up the extra fifty pounds she carried around her belly, thighs, and ass.

But Keeton knew all about her body. Even after less than forty-eight hours, he'd seen, kissed, and done the most decadent things to nearly every inch of her. And he'd made her feel beautiful while doing it.

Yes, she'd thought it was a fling at first, but somewhere along the line she'd been bitten by the love bug. Lena believed in love at first sight. She just never expected it to happen to her.

The man who'd come to visit had been talking about something she didn't fully understand. Something about Shifters and mates. It was time for her to get some answers. Even if they broke her heart. Gathering her courage, she exited the room.

Time to face the music.

Lena sucked in a breath and walked into the living room. Keeton stood up from where he'd been sitting on the lounge chair. His friend did the same from his position on the couch.

"Hello," she said, addressing the stranger. "My name is Marilena Sorelli. You can call me Lena."

She smiled and extended her hand. She was unsure what to do when he nodded but made no move to touch her. Lena dropped her hand.

"He's not being rude. He won't touch you because he knows I would not like it." Keeton explained, but she still did not understand.

He looked so tense and uncertain, her heart squeezed inside her chest.

Maybe this was difficult for both of them. Marilena was not capable of being completely cut off from others' emotions. Her empathy and sympathy were her greatest downfalls, according to her mother. Just another mark against the woman's chubby daughter.

"You wouldn't like it if he touched me? Even just to shake my hand?"

Keeton shook his head, grimacing in a way that reminded her of a young boy who'd been caught doing something wrong. He huffed out a breath and ran his fingers through his hair and back down his beard.

He looked so gorgeous with his sweats and no shirt. The fireplace was lit, and the light from the flames danced across the muscles on his arms, chest, and abdomen. She felt heat stir within her in response to his blatant masculinity, but she ignored it.

This was not the time or place. Perhaps it never would be. The thought hurt, but she was a realist. She might have fallen for him, but she never expected this to last forever. Just look at him. He was in another league entirely. A world apart from her own pitiful self.

Fuck that, she thought with a shake of her head.

If she'd been helpless against her attraction to him, he sure as shit felt something similar. No man could fake the hungry way he'd stared at her, rolls, flub, and all. Not to mention the thorough lovemaking they'd shared. He'd wanted her every bit as much as she'd wanted him. Hell, she still wanted him. What they had was extraordinary. A once in a lifetime thing. She didn't have to be a Shifter, or whatever the stranger had called them, to feel that.

"Why? Explain why you wouldn't like it? Tell me what it is I saw happen to you. Please," she whispered the last word.

"Lena, I really shouldn't," he said, looking everywhere but at her.

"Don't I deserve to know?"

"Just tell her, man," the stranger spoke up.

"What you saw is called a half-shift—"

"Pretty gnarly one too. Not every Shifter can pull that off," the other man added.

"It happens sometimes when we lose

control of our animals—"

"Animals? What are you?" Marilena whispered, eyes wide, but not with fright.

"We're Shifters, Lena. Dual natured beings who share our souls and bodies with our spirit animals. We can call them forward, swap our skin for fur. And sometimes we take on their attributes."

Lena listened patiently to his explanations. She could see the concern on his face and wondered why he should be so afraid to tell her what he was. Keeton was a marvel in this jaded and oftentimes harsh world. A genuine miracle in her eyes. Didn't he know that?

"That's why the, the growling, um,

earlier," she mumbled, cheeks burning with embarrassment as her eyes flashed to the other man who was still sitting there.

"Oh, um, excuse me," he grumbled and stood up. "My name is Niels, Niels Orson, by the way. It is very nice to meet you."

The growl coming from Keeton's lips sent Niels running into the kitchen, and Lena frowned. Forest green eyes glowing with something she could not name met hers, and her heart thudded inside her chest.

Holy shit.

She recognized something in his stare she hadn't seen before. Or if she had, she sure as hell didn't realize what she was looking at.

His animal.

And, oh my, he was beautiful.

She'd always had an active imagination and loved reading fairytales and folklore as a child. As an adult, she'd curbed that enthusiasm for fantasy. Choosing instead to direct it toward her creative pursuits with food.

"Will you show me your animal?"

"Lena, I don't think—"

"Are you dangerous?"

"Yes. Very."

"But you won't hurt me," she replied.

For whatever reason, she just seemed to know it. Keeton Grey was a Shifter.

A magical being.

Powerful.

Capable of things she could hardly

suspect. But he would never hurt her. She'd bet her life on that fact. Was about to, at any rate.

"Lena, I shift into an Eastern Mountain Lion about twice as big as any wild cougar. I don't want to scare you."

"You won't. Please?"

He seemed unsure at first, but something in the way she looked at him seemed to move him because suddenly he was standing.

"Need to make room," he growled, and slid the chair and sofa out of the way.

"This is a little hard to watch. I will understand if you close your eyes. Just remember, I won't hurt you. I couldn't."

"Okay," she said.

Keeton slid his sweatpants off his

lean hips, revealing that deliciously long, male part of him she'd worshipped with her body mere hours ago. His massive cock stirred under her stare, and the growl that escaped his lips this time was anything but hostile.

"Lena. I can't do this if you're gonna stare at me."

"Sorry," she replied, swallowing audibly.

Her cheeks were bright red. Must be, she reckoned, considering his knowing smirk. He exhaled a deep breath, closing his eyes and rolling his shoulders. Then something began to happen. That air around him took on a gossamer quality. It shimmered with tiny little lights that increased in speed as they zipped around Keeton's magnificent form.

Then he crouched, a look of pain crossed his face for one brief moment, causing her to rush forward. But by the time she reached him, Keeton was no longer Keeton. He was a five-hundred-pound Mountain Lion with six-inch fangs. Lena stopped short. Her momentum was too strong for her injured ankle to hold, and she fell backward, landing on her ass. The Keeton-Cat roared, and Niels came running, stopping in the doorway when the Mountain Lion turned and snarled at him.

"Fuck, Keeton, shut up already," he told the cat nonchalantly. "You okay? He won't hurt you. You're his mate. He couldn't if he wanted to."

"Mate? What do you mean?" Lena asked as she used the coffee table to stand.

Keeton moved forward, rubbing his head on her belly, and causing her to lean heavily on him else she fall again.

It was crazy.

Unbelievable.

And yet, she felt completely at ease with the incredible creature. The sound of his purrs made her grin, and before she knew it, she was on the couch with the gigantic animal pushing between her legs so he could embrace her in his furry form.

Holy shit.

This was really real.

And for some reason, she accepted it as a fact. Maybe it was her upbringing and the lack of magic in her childhood. Maybe it was because he was there in his fur. Right in front of her face.

LOL.

Either way. She was happy to know there was magic out there. And just maybe, some of it was for her.

His sandpapery tongue licked her cheek, and Lena giggled, stroking the big cat's fur with her hands. Laughing out loud when he licked her again.

"Alright, down!" She tried to push him, but he would not budge.

"You're crushing me, Keeton," she said with another laugh tickling her throat, and this time he moved, sitting down on his haunches directly in front of her.

Lena stopped, smiled, and just

stared at the familiar green eyes that glittered at her. His face might be different, but her heart recognized Keeton. The air surrounding his body shimmered once more, and he was a man once again. He did not look at her as he tugged on his sweatpants. Her heart squeezed inside her chest as she recognized what he was doing.

He was building a wall between them. It hurt. But she understood. She'd heard his comments to his friend earlier. Keeton Grey was not going to leave his mountain. Not even for her. And Marilena Sorelli could not stay there. She was meant for the world. Even as her heart broke, she knew the truth behind her thoughts.

"I'm going to get some more

firewood," he grumbled, moving quickly out the front door.

"Your shoes," she called after him, but he was already gone.

"He'll be okay." Niels entered the living room with a tray of tea and cookies.

He poured two cups, handing her one and sat on the couch opposite of Lena. The hot tea warmed her suddenly chilled hands. This was the most wondrous, and also the saddest two days of her life. How was she going to go back home now? After everything she'd seen and experienced?

"So, you're a Shifter too? Like Keeton?"

"Yes, and no. I am a Shifter, but not a Mountain Lion. My animal is a

Grizzly."

"Oh, I see. So what are you guys exactly?"

"What do you mean?"

"Well, are you cursed? Like Werewolves? Or are you like Aliens or something?"

"No," he answered, snorting into his teacup. "We're humans with a little something extra in our DNA. The government called it a mutation, but there is magic in our blood. Hell, there is magic in the entire world, but normals, that's what we call humans, don't readily recognize it anymore."

"I guess that's true. But you said something else to Keeton earlier. You called me his mate. What does that mean?"

"Oh, uh, Lena, he should probably explain it to you."

"But he won't. You know he won't."

Niels placed his cup on the coffee table, seeming to ponder her question. He was huge, a little scary, and did not at all put her at ease the way Keeton's presence seemed to. But she knew she was safe. Keeton would not have left her otherwise.

Whatever wonderful magical mystery she'd stumbled upon in Panther Mountains, she needed the entire story. It would help her understand it all when she returned home.

"First, you have to know that this is a secret."

"But the government knows—"

"Yeah," he growled. "They know

about a lot of stuff they don't tell the public. But for your good, and ours, the Shifter secret must be kept."

"Of course," she promised. "I won't tell a soul."

"I believe you. Shifters can sense emotions. I know you will keep Keeton's secret because I know you love him."

"What? How can you? Does he?" She gulped audibly.

"He probably can sense it, but he is in denial. Have you ever heard of *fated mates*?"

Lena shook her head. She leaned forward and placed her mug on the table. Patience wasn't her fortitude, but she needed every ounce in her possession, and Niels chose his words carefully. Each second that passed with

Keeton gone, she felt his absence more and more keenly.

What could that be if not love or magic?

And who was to say one existed without the other?

She shook her head. She was being silly. Even so, she wanted information, and the Bear was sitting on a goldmine.

"Tell me," she demanded.

"In Shifter lore, there is a legend, one soul created for another, one body designed to fit one mate, one being meant for one other alone. *Fated mates*, you understand? As rare and valuable as anything in this realm or any other. Each Shifter is born with a one in a million shot at finding his or her fated mate. I believe you are Keeton's."

"I am?"

Niels nodded, his face as serious as a heart attack. Marilena gasped. She covered her mouth with her hands. This was incredible. If she was Keeton's fated mate, then he wouldn't just let her disappear. Would he?

"Yes." Keeton's voice sounded from behind her.

Surprising her so that she jumped and knocked her knee into the coffee table, disrupting the tea set. Happiness swelled inside of her, but he didn't return her smile. He stood still, skin glistening with wet from the elements.

"You're my fated mate, Lena, but I am no good for you. The storm passed. Tomorrow, I'll take you home."

"But—" She wanted to argue, but the

set of his shoulders and the way he turned his face stopped her in her tracks.

"Fine," she replied in a small voice.

"But you needn't bother yourself. Niels will take me home. Right?" she asked the big man, who nodded his head, watching Keeton warily out of the corner of his eye.

"Fine. Whatever you want," Keeton growled.

"No," she replied. "Never that. If you will excuse me."

Marilena turned around and went back to the bedroom. It was his, and she had no right to it, but she was not about to sleep on the couch after everything she'd been through.

Fated mate?

No.

It must be a mistake.

She did not believe for a moment she was his fated mate.

If it were true, how could he let her go so easily?

Lena tried not to think about it, but it was no use. She sat up all night long, waiting for daybreak. When she finally packed and dressed for the long trek down the mountain, keeping his thermal on beneath her sweater and jacket, she exited Keeton's bedroom.

I'm not gonna cry.

Not gonna cry.

She repeated the mantra as she walked into the living room and looked around. But it was empty.

"He left," Niels said from the kitchen.

“Oh. I guess he didn’t want to say goodbye.”

Niels shrugged. He looked upset but smiled pleasantly. Niels took her bag from her and walked outside.

“We will have to go slow. I twisted my ankle and—”

Before she could finish her thought, Niels was pulling a tarp off a muddy, but functional UTV. He grinned and gestured for her to slide into the passenger seat.

“Hell! You didn’t think I walked here, did you? I’ll have you know I really am smarter than the average Bear.” Niels winked playfully, and Lena laughed. Neither of them caught sight of the forest green eyes watching from the rooftop or heard the mournful yowling of

Keeton's Mountain Lion.

"Come on. We'll be down the mountain in no time at all," Niels said.

"Okay," Lena said, her heart breaking as she slid into the cold leather seat.

They'd only gotten half the promised snow, and even that had already started to melt. It didn't matter. The large tires of the Utility Terrain Vehicle moved easily over the snow, rocks, and mud.

Lena would just have to forget her time up there on Panther, make that *Shifter* Mountain. She'd tuck it away like every other secret little dream she'd ever had. Safe and sound, something for her to pull out when she was all alone so she could remember and relive her time with him.

The first man to ever touch her heart.

CHAPTER TEN

"GET UP!" NIELS kicked at his foot, and Keeton snarled angrily.

It had been three weeks since she'd gone, taking all the sunshine with her. He'd done his best since then to drink himself into a stupor. The empty bottles littering his once pristine floor were evidence of that.

"The fuck, bro?" Keeton bolted up off the carpet after Niels dumped a cup of icy cold water on his head.

"You asshole. Still sitting here, then. What are you doing, Keeton? Waiting for another mate to knock on your door and fall in your lap? You sorry sonofabitch!" Niels sneered, shoving Keeton into the wall.

He roared in retaliation, tackling his blood brother, *one of his best friends*, down to the ground. Niels responded in kind. The two men well matched in skin, even with his days of wallowing in drink and misery. They wrestled and punched their way across the living room, busting up some of his furniture in the process.

But who gave a fuck?

What did it matter when he had no one to share it with anyway?

"What kind of jerk are you, bro? She was special. Lena was perfect for you. And you let her go!"

"I had no choice! You know what I did, Niels. I couldn't risk exposing her to my own lack of control!"

"Bullshit! Bruce Taylor was a fucking lowlife. You are not responsible for that asshole's death," Niels snarled in outrage.

"He didn't trust me. What if she doesn't? What if she can't?"

"Some shit is worth the risk. Don't you think you owe it to the both of you to try? Fuck man, if I met my mate, you could be damn sure I wouldn't give her up for anything, let alone fear. You are braver than you give yourself credit for, Keeton. And you're a good man too."

"She deserves better."

"Damn straight." Niels chuckled. "But she loves you. Unfortunately, you might be too late."

"What do you mean?"

He sat up, pushing the Bear away from him as fear gripped his heart. Yes, the last few weeks had been hell. But somewhere deep inside, he thought he still had a shot. Niels' next words were about to put a serious damper on that.

"She's preparing for a wedding right now."

The big man dropped that bomb a little too nonchalantly, but Keeton was too amped up to notice. Nor did he see the grin Niels hid behind his hand.

"Where is she?" Keeton growled, unable to keep the Lion from his voice.

"In Maccon City. At the new Oasis Convention Center behind their beachside hotel."

"Keys! Now!"

"Fuck, man, take a shower first. You stink. Besides, ceremony isn't till seven."

Keeton looked down with wild eyes.

A shower?

Fuck.

He did stink.

He showered and dressed quickly. His frown increased when he saw Niels waiting in the driver's side of his UTV.

"I can drive myself."

"Maybe, but this is my vehicle, fuck

you very much. Besides, I know a shortcut. Hold on."

***

"Lena, here are the dried rose petals you asked for," Bobby, her newly hired assistant, said, handing her the package of edible flowers.

"Thanks." She smiled.

Things were really looking up for her now. It was Halloween, her favorite holiday, and the sun was shining. Lena had been hired to cater a themed wedding at the Oasis Convention Center in Maccon City, her new hometown, and she was delighted with the menu.

The bride and groom had decided on a very nontraditional dessert table with two hundred champagne flutes filled with *Mahalabia*, the specialty pudding made of rosewater and milk she once told Keeton about.

Dammit.

Don't think about him.

She refocused on her task at hand, admiring the finished pudding. She'd dyed it a blood red color per the bride's request, and it was the centerpiece of the dessert table. Decadent dark and white chocolate Petit fours sat on either side on two three-tiered trays, and she'd written the happy couple's names with the white on an extra long bar of the dark chocolate. Lena had even molded a bride and groom with little skeleton faces for them.

She used dried roses and pistachios as garnish on the bar and all three desserts, along with edible gold and silver flakes appropriate for the celebration. The results were beyond her expectations, and she felt pride in a job well done. Looking down at her soiled chef coat, she made a mental note to change before the evening began.

She was not serving, but she would stay in the kitchen to direct the proper heating and serving of the food. There would, of course, be a cocktail hour, followed by a pasta course, then four carving stations and a buffet of sides would be set up in the main room.

She'd prepared a rosemary and garlic infused prime rib roast, a Cajun-style deep-fried turkey, a smoked ham, and two hundred lump-crab cakes with a spicy remoulade on the side. It was hard work, but she loved it, and hoped her clients would be happy.

If only the rest of her life was falling in line as smoothly as this dinner, she thought with a sad sigh. Whatever. She had no reason to complain. After she'd returned to the hotel on well-salted New Jersey roads, she sank into a depression she wasn't sure she could shake. But a visit from her mother the very next day had woken her up.

"Mom! What are you doing here? And you brought Cary with you?" She stomped her foot angrily at the two of them standing in her doorway.

"Good God, child! Where on earth have you been?"

"Yes, Marilena, we were so worried."

Cary attempted to reach out, but the

thought of him touching her made her skin crawl. She stepped back, shaking her head angrily.

"Cary? Get out of my room!"

"Lena! You have no call to be rude to him. Especially not after I begged him to give you another chance—"

"Me? Mom, he cheated on me! With his secretary! I do not need or want a chance with him—"

"Lena! Be reasonable, who else will take you with your weight issue."

"Oh my God, Mom, you know what, I am so done with this conversation. I need both of you to leave. Now!"

"You will not speak to me this way. I am your mother."

"Are you? Cause you treat me like a goddamned burden, Mom. I never felt

your approval or love once in my whole life. Do you know that? Do you even see how you hurt me time and again with your cruel and thoughtless words?"

"Oh, Lena. No, I just..." Her mother's eyes widened as she stumbled over her words. She clutched her hands to her chest and then, narrowing her hazel eyes at Cary, the older woman did something that shocked the hell out of her daughter.

"Cary, get the hell out of here, you sniveling little wretch! You never deserved my daughter. Shame on you for being so predictable! Shtupping the secretary? Really? Oh, leave already," she said, and pushed him out the door.

"Mom! Did you really just do that?" Lena snorted, covering her mouth.

"Marilena, I'm sorry if I have been

hard on you. I just want the best for you. I might be a hard person, lord knows your father thought so, but he loved you and so do I. Very much. I'd like you to come home, Lena."

"Thank you, Mom. I love you too. But I think I am fine right where I am."

"Are you sure? Alright then. Call me when you are settled. I'd like to see you. When you have time, of course."

"Okay," she said, hugging her mother for the first time since she was a child.

It was the first time in a long while that she felt close to her only living parent. Seeing Cary had been a shock, but her total lack of feeling for the man was evident. She should have thanked him for cheating on her, she thought with a giggle.

The sound of shouting reached her all the way in the kitchen, and for just a second, Lena swore she recognized the person's voice. But it couldn't be him. Keeton wouldn't come after her. Not after all this time. The yelling increased, followed by a long animalistic snarl.

Uh oh.

She ran toward the front of the building where a security guard was currently locked in full nelson by the man who'd just broken her heart.

"Keeton, for fuck's sake, they're normals here!" The guard, whom she knew as Alex, had glowing gold eyes.

"You're a Shifter too?" Lena asked, surprised.

"Fuck! Tell your mate to get a grip," the guard said, and something about him reminded her of a dog, or Wolf.

“Lena,” Keeton said, tossing the man to the floor like he was nothing more than a rag doll.

He stepped into her space, not touching, but the way his eyes roamed over her from head to toe was just as intimate. She swallowed audibly, choking on the sob that threatened to reveal itself. What was he doing here? Why was he looking at her like she was a drink of water and he’d been stranded in the desert, dying for a sip?

“Cause I have been,” he whispered, reaching out with long-fingered hands to pull her into his hard body. “I’m dying without you, Lena. Love you, mate, missed you.”

Keeton wrapped her in the warmth of

his steel embrace. Choking on emotion, he kissed her hair, her head, finally, her lips. She sighed, tasting the tears as they rolled down her cheeks and into their kiss. But it didn't matter. Nothing did except him.

"You're here? You came down from your mountain. Why?"

"Because I love you. I was wrong to let you go. Please don't get married. Not to anyone but me. I can't live without you, Marilena."

"Good, because I don't want to live without you. But Keeton, I'm not getting married."

"What?" He turned abruptly, and she followed his line of sight to find Niels standing there grinning from ear to ear.

"I told you." He turned to face Lena

with a goofy grin on his face. "I'm smarter than the average Bear."

He winked and left before Keeton could go after him. Lena laughed aloud, hugging her ornery Mountain Lion tight. He growled, lifting her off the ground and spinning her in a circle.

"So," she said as he lowered her to her feet, raining kisses on her face and mouth. "Do you mean it? Are you staying here, in the real world, with me?"

"Yes, I mean it."

"But what about your mountain?"

"I suppose it will keep. We can go there on weekends when we need a little quiet."

"I think I'd like that," she whispered, sealing her lips to his.

"Let's get out of here," he growled and flexed his hips, allowing her to feel the evidence of his fierce arousal.

"I'd like that, but, you see, I'm working," she said, gnawing her lower lip worriedly.

The last thing she wanted was for Keeton to think she did not want him. But she had been hired to do a job, and this was her business. Surely the mountain man would understand. She waited for him to speak.

"I don't suppose you could use a *sous chef*?"

Lena gasped, delighting in his green eyes that sparkled with love as he placed a hand on her waist and guided her back to the kitchen.

A *sous chef*?

What a wonderful idea!

"I would love it," she replied.

Together they worked side by side, a precursor of their lives together, she realized with wonder and pure joy filling her with each passing moment. Keeton was already an excellent cook. He listened to her instructions and surprised her with some innovative methods of his own. He wasn't classically trained, but as he explained, Shifters had very acute senses. His senses, mainly taste and smell, could decipher far more complex flavors than a human's. Made him a natural born chef.

"I just might hire you full time," she said, only half-joking after tasting his homemade remoulade.

"I think I'd love working with you permanently, Chef Sorelli."

The deep purr in his throat held promises she could hardly wait for.

"Later, mate," he said, catching her lips in a hard, quick kiss before turning his attention back to the croquettes.

"Show me once more how to pack them so they don't break."

"Okay," she smiled, going back to work.

***

Keeton closed the door to the house his sweet mate had been renting for the past few weeks. It was a nice and tidy little Victorian on a cul-de-sac that afforded them some privacy, though not as much as his cabin.

That was alright with him, though. He didn't need to run and hide from the world. Not anymore. The past few hours had been sweet torture working next to his unclaimed mate while she smiled and greeted those wedding guests who wanted to meet the head chef at the event.

Shifters did not particularly like sharing. And yet, because he knew she was his, his Mountain Lion did not object. At least, not out loud. The drive to her house was fast, but even seconds were too long. He wanted her. His cat did too. The need to claim the sweet woman who'd haunted every single moment since he'd first seen her on the mountain was growing stronger by the minute.

"Come on." She tugged on his hand, and he went with her as docile as a kitten. "This is why I chose to rent this house. You know, I have an option to buy from the owner," she said, biting her lip as she turned the shower on.

Keeton was tongue-tied, watching his gorgeous mate as she stripped off her clothes and walked backward into the stall. The three showerheads that lined the walls all sprayed simultaneously, drenching her hair, and sluicing down her beautiful and oh-so-tempting body.

"Well?" She summoned him with a curl of her finger, and he almost walked in with his clothes still on.

"Fuck," he growled, getting tangled in his jeans as he tried unsuccessfully to unbutton the fly.

Fuck it.

Keeton unleashed his claws, shredding the thick denim and doing the same to his shirt. Lucky for his boots, they slid off with no problem. Lena watched him, mouth open, but he saw no trace of fear or disgust. His idiotic, animalistic display actually heightened her arousal.

The sweet, honey-rose scent infiltrated his nostrils, going straight to his ever-hardening dick. Keeton was through waiting. He stepped onto the wet tiles, closing the sliding shower door behind him.

"Finally," she murmured, pulling him to her deliciously wet skin. Her taught nipples dug into his chest, and he purred deep in his throat.

"Lena," he whispered. Burying his hands in her wet hair, he angled her head and lowered his until his mouth was crushing hers beneath his kiss, so full of unbridled passion, he damn near shook with the force of it.

His mate nestled in closer to him with a deep sigh of longing, one he felt all the way to his toes.

Fuck, she was gorgeous.

So beautiful, so trusting, he thought, amazed, as he lifted her up in his arms and backed her up against the tiled wall.

Lena's hands clutched at his shoulders as she wrapped her legs around his waist, bringing her heated core into direct contact with his hard-as-fuck cock. Keeton growled in response to the helpless flex of her hips. The tiny movements, so soft and slow, tortured them both.

"Want you. Want to claim you, mate," he growled into her mouth, swallowing her responding moan.

The constant sensual brushing of her hot, wet pussy against his shaft was making him lose control. But instead of running from it, he embraced it. Keeton understood better than ever that his beast was part of him, as surely as Lena was. The animal would never harm her, or him, for that matter. He simply needed to be present for this.

Mine.

Mate.

Yes, he told the cat, soothing the creature with a promise that tonight he was going to claim her.

"Please, Keeton," she murmured, flexing her hips against him once more.

"Need you to tell me you want this."

"I want this. I want you. Make me yours," she begged.

Keeton's heart thudded roughly inside his chest, so hard it thought it beat right out of him. She was a treasure. His one and only, and he was going to do right by her or die trying.

"Mine," he growled with all the fierceness of his beast.

Flexing his hips, he entered her in one swift motion, dragging a moan from her sweet lips. One after the other, growls and tension built as he moved within her heat. His Lena tested his control like no other. She bucked against him in time with his thrusts, trusting him to hold her safe and secure in the wet shower.

He could do that.

And so much more.

He shifted his position, angling her so that her back was on the wall and her hips thrust forward. Keeton felt himself slide deeper inside her heated slit. His fingers tightened on her ass as he lifted her and slammed her back down on his cock. Loving the moans and pants that escaped her lips as she fought for her pleasure, the same way he fought to give it to her.

Her smooth, silky skin glistened like opals under the spray of water. So tempting, so soft. He couldn't wait to sink his teeth there, just above her breast. To mark her with his bite, bind her to him, and finally stake his claim.

His Mountain Lion was riding him hard, demanding he strike now. But not yet. He needed her to come first.

"Keeton," she moaned his name.

Her breath was coming in quick, hard gusts, and he knew she was close. Could feel it in the way her walls tightened on his cock. Fuck, she was squeezing him so damn hard.

Felt so good.

Incredible.

"Mine," he snarled, increasing his pace.

Bolts of pleasure shot through his body, lighting his nervous system on fire. Lena moaned, a deep and guttural sound, and he struck just as her pussy squeezed him. His Lion roared loudly as he swallowed her life's force, the honey taste of her blood coating his throat. He swallowed a mouthful as she came around his cock, taking her with him into the height of ecstasy.

Even as he came, spilling his semen deep within her womb, Keeton kept pistoning his hips. Her sex began to ripple and tighten once more, urging her into her second orgasm as he licked her wounds closed with his healing saliva.

This was only the beginning of what would be a raucous night of lovemaking and claiming. He couldn't wait, he thought with a satisfied growl as he lifted his well-sexed and fully claimed mate out of the shower stall. Grabbing two fluffy towels from the shelf, he carried her to the bed.

"Love you," she whispered with a small smile teasing the corner of her kiss swollen lips.

"I love you too, mate," he said, and proceeded to show her.

Keeton made love to Lena throughout the night. Taking her again, and again, and again, and still, he was insatiable as he collapsed onto her body after their fourth round.

"Oh wow," she gasped, struggling to breathe.

"Did I hurt you?" He lifted his head, concern glowing in his green haze.

"No, of course not. But Keeton," she said as he rolled onto his side, rearranging her exhausted limbs so she would be comfortable.

"What, sweet?"

"I think we should buy this house."

He started laughing then. Holding her face between his hands, he kissed her nose.

"I had that same exact thought the second I watched you step into that shower."

"And you mean it about working with me? At *Happy Ever After Events & Catering LLC*?"

"If you are willing to hire me, yes, I'd love it."

"Of course."

"There's just one thing," he said, kissing her head and pulling her on top of him.

Lena's eyes widened when she wiggled her hips and his cock rose to attention, hardening beneath her silky sex. The scent of her arousal now carried with it notes of his Lion. He growled with pleasure, loving that she would wear his mark and carry his scent with her always.

"What thing?" she asked. Lena sat up. Rotating her hips slowly, she slid her dripping pussy up and down, over his shaft so that his eyes rolled to the back of his head.

"Marry me, Lena? Be mine in the human world as well as the Shifter one?"

"Yes, my love, oh yes," she said, lifting her hips up so she could take him inside once more.

This time, their lovemaking was slow and thorough. A body long slide of skin against skin, souls against souls. He could feel it, could feel her through their matebond and it shook him to the marrow.

“Keeton, I feel you,” she whispered, eyes closed, and lips open as she made love to him with everything she had inside.

“I know, mate,” he purred, rolling them over, so he was on top, in control, guiding their lovemaking through unknown territory.

“I feel you too, Lena. You’re in my blood, in my soul, in my heart.”

“Oh, Keeton.”

“I love you, Marilena.”

He increased the speed, the power behind his thrusts until he felt her squeezing him exactly right. His balls tightened, cock aching with the need to come, then he did. Simultaneously, they reached new heights, bodies arching, jerking in their passion.

"I love you, my mountain man. I am gonna try so hard to make this place a home for you," she said, exhaling as she clutched him tight to her breast.

"You're my home, Lena, no matter where we are. It's always been you," he replied and felt the truth of that statement as the last bit of that stone wall he once had erected around his heart shattered.

Stone was no match for the strength of his love for her. She was his everything.

His only thing.

His fated mate.

And he would spend the rest of his life loving her. That was a promise he intended to keep.

EPILOGUE

KEETON AND MARILENA were married just before Thanksgiving, having closed on that mid-size Victorian house only days before. They chose to honeymoon up at the cabin since they needed to close it up before the winter months hit the Garden state.

Niels had been the best man, with Silas an usher for the ceremony. Only a handful of guests were invited, as the couple chose to keep the celebration intimate. It was time for the Bear to get on the road, anyway. He had more of the world to see, more to taste.

"Where are you heading now, Niels?" Silas stalked toward him with all the majestic grace of the large African Lion that resided inside of him.

How he could stand living in a city was beyond Niels, but whatever. To each his own. He accepted the cold longneck and nodded his thanks.

"Don't know. Winter is hard up here, thought I'd go try my luck down in South America for a while."

"I see," Silas replied, but his gaze

kept going back to the cute blonde administrative assistant he'd brought with him as his plus one.

"What about you? Going back to your corporate coffin?"

"Don't knock it," the other man shrugged.

"Yeah, yeah. What are you two pussies doing out here?" Keeton walked out onto the porch where his two blood brothers sat.

"First off, you two are the pussies. I'm a motherfucking Grizzly," Niels corrected, leaving Silas to snort into his bottle.

"Yeah, right," Keeton replied, still smiling. He offered the big man a hand before sitting down. "I owe you one, man. If it wasn't for you, I might have let Lena walk out of my life. I can't ever repay you—"

"No need," Niels replied, shaking his head.

"This big fucker is leaving again," Silas said, ratting him out.

"Is that true?"

"Yeah, I'll be back, though. In the summer, maybe."

"Alright. But you better promise. For some reason, my Lena likes you," he said.

"Ha. And I thought her taste was questionable cause she married you. Now I know it's just bad," Silas joked, but Keeton growled threateningly.

"Just a joke, man."

"A bad one."

"Ha ha. We'll see how you feel once

you realize you're in love with the tidbit you brought with you, tough guy," Niels said, outing his buddy.

"The fuck you say!" Silas stood up, slamming his bottle on the table.

"Hey! Knock it off, it's my wedding day. Assholes." Keeton shook his head. Catching his new bride's eye from inside the doorway, he excused himself to be with her.

"You don't know shit," Silas growled, stalking off into the cold night while Niels just sat there with his beer.

It wasn't easy being the only one of his three comrades to have zero attachment to anyone. Silas might be fighting it, but Niels knew him. Maybe better than he knew himself. That blonde meant something to the big man.

Figured his two feline friends had mates, and he didn't.

"Guess fated mates are for pussies." He shrugged, not even bothering to laugh at his own bad joke.

Of course, the Fates weren't at all happy with that assumption as they watched the Grizzly from the heavens above. In fact, they just might have to prove him wrong.

Thanks for reading!

***

The Hearts of Stone Series by C.D. Gorri will continue with Shifter City and Shifter Village. Look for them both here in 2022.

Turn the page for a preview from Shifter City, Hearts of Stone, Book Two!

PREVIEW

Will her love break through his heart of stone?

Silas McKennon is a corporate shark, er, Lion. All business, this hard-hearted male hates women. He simply refuses to have anything to do with them.

Well, except for one.

SHIFTER MOUNTAIN

Blonde and brainy, Larissa Clark works for Silas as his right hand man, er, woman. She's a sharp shooting administrative assistant and one of the few females he will tolerate.

Having the hots for her hunky boss is just one of the secrets she has to keep in order to stay in the city she loves. When the prince of the local Pride starts pursuing Larissa, she has no choice but to skip town.

But Silas is not ready to let his prized employee go. He'll do anything to stop it, including mate her.

Will she risk it all on a man whose heart is made of stone?

PROLOGUE

Years ago…

SHOTS RANG OUT and Silas ducked for cover behind the thick stand of trees, all that separated him from the line of men firing unscrupulously into the forest.

His Lion's eyes searched through the darkness and found his two brothers in arms, Keeton Grey and Niels Orson. The three of them were hired soldiers, mercenaries for lack of a better word. After a stint in the armed forces, none of them had been ready to go back to the real world.

Him especially.

Returning to the big city to deal with his mother's illness, his deceased father's lawyers, and the floundering company that was his legacy and heritage, did not appeal in the least to him or his Lion. He'd much rather roam the world, righting wrongs and punishing those who deserved it.

But this last job hadn't gone according to plan. It wasn't always easy to discern who was just and who was in the wrong. Silas had been a fool to think otherwise.

The female operative who'd run a counter game on their unit had taken him in more than most. She was sweet and smart with a svelte body and a killer smile. She was to be their liaison in the small village they'd come to free from a modern warlord's rule.

Of course, Silas hadn't been aware of her exploits with others in his unit until after he'd let her into his bed. Lola Yen was a full human who was not aware of his other half when he'd allowed the Asian beauty to seduce him after they'd been briefed on their assignment.

That was why she hadn't understood how he knew she'd been with someone else. Turned out, she was in bed with the warlord they came to overthrow and had led them into an ambush.

Lucky for Silas, Keeton, and Niels, the three Shifters had sniffed out the danger, so to speak. She'd come to him right before they shoved out, the stink of a human male all over her tawny skin. He knew then they were being played and had informed his team.

Lola had been taken into custody, and his heart had hardened to stone. Just like that. They had come there to do a job, and they were going to finish it, dammit. But afterward, he was done.

This was going to be Silas' last operation.

If he made it out alive, he thought grimly.

Fuck that.

He shook his head. Silas would make

it out alive. He had to see his mother. Had to take back the company that his dad had left him. Yeah, he was gonna survive. Niels and Keeton too. That was a motherfucking promise.

He saw the questioning look in Keeton's eyes before Silas shook his head. He was furious at himself for so easily believing the deception that brought them to that point.

"I'm gonna shift," he whispered, knowing they could both hear him over the din of gunfire. From one minute to the next, he swapped skin for golden fur, and his nine-hundred-pound African Lion emerged. Silently, he stalked around the scraggly group of soldiers until he was in the right position. Then he roared, scaring the literal piss out of them.

The men screamed, dropping weapons, and running for their lives. Of course, Keeton and Niels were there to round them up. And when they gave up the warlord's position, they claimed they had to because the *King Lion* was hunting them for their evil ways.

King Lion.

He snorted whenever he thought of the nickname, but his beast liked it just fine. After all, Silas was an Alpha, a king in his own right. He shook his head.

Nah.

He was just a man. And that was enough for now.

Roar.

Stay tuned in for more about the Hearts of Stone Series, and other steamy PNR tales here:

https://www.cdgorri.com

Signup to my newsletter and get a free copy of **Charley's Christmas Wolf**...

https://www.cdgorri.com/newsletter

Excerpt from Code Wolf

"Are you fuckin' with me?" "No, Randall, I assure you I am not fuckin' with you," Rafe Maccon eased his immense frame back into his oversized, black leather chair and narrowed his ice blue eyes at his Third and one of his oldest friends. How long had he known the man sitting in front of him?

Randall had come to Maccon City when Rafe was about ten, he looked the same then as he did now. Tall at six foot three inches, muscular, and more than a little intimidating to the Wolves under him with his long beard and equally long dark brown hair.

Rafe, however, was the Alpha. He was

more amused than intimidated by his surly friend.

"A vacation?! What the fuck am I gonna do on a vacation? Come on, Rafe, this is bullshit!"

The door to Rafe's private office flew open and in strolled a very happy, very pregnant Charley Maccon, Rafe's wife. The Alpha's eyes glowed as they landed on his positively glowing mate. She wore a long, flowy dress. The shade was a pale-yellow color that, Randall admitted to himself, looked damn good with her creamy complexion and curly dark hair.

Their Alpha Female was quite something. There wasn't a Wolf Guard in the place who wouldn't lay down his/her life for her.

"Well, maybe you should consider a

vacation to be a relaxing experience, Randy," she dropped a kiss on Randall's cheek and walked past him, over to her husband whom she kissed full on the mouth.

The way his Alpha's eyes homed in on her when she opened the door was nothing compared to the hungry gaze that followed her across the room.

Randall had noticed it took a while for Rafe to get used to his mate's habit of greeting everyone with a kiss or hug. Wolves were protective of their mates, but Randall thought his Alpha was doing an exceedingly good job of hiding his tension. Werewolves did not share very well.

Charley; however, had stood firm. That was the way she was raised, and she wasn't going to change for any, how had she put it? Neanderthal brow beating husband, regardless of how cute his ass was!

Randall had no direct knowledge if the "cute ass" statement was true or not. And he didn't want to know. He liked Charley though, had from the beginning. He was musically inclined and often took to one of the common rooms to strum his guitar or play a few keys on the piano.

Excerpt from Grizzly Lover

"Resa," Oliver fisted the note he'd found tucked under the secondhand keyboard he'd just finished paying off.

The instrument sat against one wall of the cramped room, right beside the only window in the small Brooklyn Heights apartment he'd been renting the past six months since he came to the city.

For a Grizzly Bear Shifter used to the wilds of the woods as his backyard, it was quite the change, but he just had to try to see if he could make a go of his music. Oliver had always been gifted with a good ear, but even as a cub, his mother had encouraged him to go and seek his destiny.

Brooklyn Heights was as close to Manhattan as he could afford with his meager savings, but what did money matter anyway? Especially when there was music to be written. The window faced the south brick wall of another small apartment complex identical to his.

It didn't matter what it looked like outside, as long as he was able to breathe some fresh air. At least on the fifth floor, it was somewhat fresher than the heavily congested streets below.

She was gone. His mind registered that fact as he took in the empty room. She'd left.

"No," he growled, and aimed his fist at the tiled counter top, cracking a few of the old ceramic squares in the process.

Mrs. Goldstein, the landlady, would be pissed when she saw that.

Oliver's Bear roared inside of him and his heart contracted painfully in his chest. It was worse than being sucker punched by Thor his idiot cousin, who was as big and strong as his namesake. Why would Teresa say such cruel things? He couldn't believe it, couldn't fathom his sweet Resa saying such foul callous words about their relationship. He read the hated missive one more time.

Oliver,

It was fun while it lasted, but even you can't be so naïve as to think I could find true love with a nobody. I just wanted to get back at my father. Don't bother looking for me or calling, I will have already changed my number.

Teresa

Yes, it was her handwriting. He closed his eyes on the wave of anguish that washed over him. Gasping, he sunk to his knees while the beast inside of him roared and stomped his massive claws in fury.

Mate, his Bear cried out, but Oliver refused to answer his other half.

How could she just leave him like this? He'd been so sure of her, of them. He was positive that she loved him too. Being with her was everything to him. She was his fated mate. It was the first time he had ever tasted happiness. A taste that was bitter now that he knew it was all one-sided.

The first time he'd seen the golden-haired beauty, Oliver's Grizzly Bear had stood up and taken notice. The second he'd breathed in her peaches and cream scent, his animal had roared one single word in his mind's eye that would change Oliver's life forever.

Mate.

Following his heart, he'd approached the soft spoken, elegantly dressed Teresa Witherspoon after spying her at the park day after day. She'd sit on one of the cleaner benches and read from a book of seventeenth century cavalier poets.

"You like Lovelace? Looking at you I pictured a Donne fan," Oliver said when he'd finally found the nerve to approach her.

"Spiritualist poetry doesn't appeal as

much to me I guess. I like Lovelace and Suckling. They're fun and witty."

"But they're just trying to get in a girl's pants with their poetry. You approve?" he grinned.

"It's not so much the seduction that appeals to me, it's the living in the moment. Carpe diem and all that," she shrugged.

There was something so tragically sad about her that his heart had squeezed in his chest with longing. He'd wanted to make her smile. Heck, he even pretended to stumble in the grass, laid himself flat just to get her to walk over and touch him. And she had, put her soft, long hands right on him to see if he was alright. He'd stolen a kiss and had never looked back. Until now. The dream was over. She'd left him.

Oliver's Bear roared in his grief. That last night they were together, he'd told her the truth about what he was. The fact that there were more things in the world than she had ever imagined.

Oliver Pax had committed a most grievous sin against his Clan. He'd confessed to a normal, a human woman, that he was a Grizzly Bear Shifter.

It was allowed under certain circumstances, like when the woman in question was your fated mate. He'd thought she'd taken it well, after all, they'd made wild, passionate love immediately after. Hell, he'd been so caught up in the moment, he'd marked her with his bite, tying himself to her irrevocably, but now she was gone.

What would become of him? Would he go mad like so many other Shifters who'd lost their mates? He had heard the stories. The tales of broken matings and rogue Shifters who needed to be put down.

Oliver tipped the bottle of whiskey back emptying its fiery contents down his throat. Then he threw the hated thing across the room. Something about the muted violence of the act satisfied his animal's need for savagery. The Bear inside of him wanted to tear the whole world down, but maybe work would be a better outlet, he thought.

Oliver sat down at his banged-up keyboard and began to play. He poured out his bruised heart. Wrote lyrics and tied them together with a fairy tale as old as they come. The Beast of Brooklyn Heights was born that day. And the rest, as they say, was history.

Excerpt from Breaking Sass

Goddammit, Sheila Rand pulled her Soft-'Vert over on the shoulder of the four lane highway. She'd been out for a spin on her bike alone after closing up the bar to try and weed out the negative thoughts and worries that had plagued her throughout the day.

This was her favorite thing about Blue Creek, the new place of residence for the Dire Wolf Motorcycle Club. The Pack she'd chosen to run with as a young woman had been a group of renegades and nomads like all Dire Wolves were. Only, they'd decided to end the cycle. The fact that they usually attracted unwanted attention in the form of challenges because of their size and strength kept the small number of elusive Shifters on the road. That and riding a motorcycle was just fucking fun.

Derrick, her cousin and their Alpha, had a nose for things. When he'd announced his plans to settle, the whole lot of them had agreed to join him. Tired of life on the road, they wanted roots, they wanted a home. So, here she was.

With their Alpha just mated, the rest of their small Pack of Dire Wolves had begun to hope that they too would find their fated mates in the small American town. All except for Sheila. She was perfectly fine on her own, and she didn't need a man to complete her, or whatever horseshit those graybeards of her old Pack had tried to convince her of when she'd been just a cub.

She could deal with the sighs and whines of the lovesick men whom she'd pledged to ride, and land, with. Overgrown cubs, the whole bunch of them. Crying in their beers about needing a mate. The Pack was in Blue Creek to stay and that meant she was too. But she'd never signed on to deal with *him.*

Nuh uh. Not her. She looked in her rearview mirror at the sedan that was pulled over onto the shoulder behind her with one end sticking slightly into the traffic lane, to protect the person being hassled of course, and the customary siren perched on the roof. Lights flashing, at least the bastard didn't turn on the sound.

He'd been waiting on her of course. Fucking speed traps should be illegal. What harm was she doing taking her frustrations out on the road when no one else in their right mind was out and about?

No one except him.

Her supposed fated mate stepped out of his vehicle and walked up to Sheila.

"Take your helmet off," he said in his gruff voice.

"Make me," she countered.

"Sheila," his tone held a warning note, but she didn't give a fuck.

"Detective," she countered.

"It's dangerous on the road at night," he started.

"For you maybe, but I was born on the

road, detective. Just one more difference between you and me. Now, you giving me a ticket?"

"Not tonight," he said, "get home safe."

She ignored his parting words, revved her engine, and shot off like a bat out of hell. Fuck. The reason for all her attitude could have been that her she-Wolf was up in arms over the man.

Mine.

No.

Grrr.

Quit it, she snapped at the Wolf inside her. Fate might have decided Detective Leo Crowley was the one for her, but Sheila wasn't about to go down without a fight.

MORE FROM C.D. GORRI

Website

Twitter

Bookbub

Instagram

FB Author Page

TikTok

***

If you enjoyed this book, you may also

enjoy...

YA Urban Fantasy Books

Macconwood Pack Novel Series

Macconwood Pack Tales

The Falk Clan Tales

The Bear Claw Tales

The Barvale Clan Tales

Purely Paranormal Pleasures

The Wardens of Terra

The Maverick Pride Tales

Dire Wolf Mates

Wyvern Protection Unit

EveL Worlds

The Guardians of Chaos

Howls Romance

Standalones

Barvale Holiday Tales

Anthologies

ABOUT THE AUTHOR

C.D. Gorri is a USA Today Bestselling and Award-Winning author of steamy paranormal romance and urban fantasy. She is the creator of the Grazi Kelly Universe. Join her mailing list here:
https://www.cdgorri.com/newsletter

An avid reader with a profound love for books and literature, when she is not writing or taking care of her family, she can usually be found with a book or tablet in hand. C.D. lives in her home state of New Jersey where many of her characters or stories are based. Her tales are fast paced yet detailed with satisfying conclusions.

If you enjoy powerful heroines and loyal heroes who face relatable problems in supernatural settings, journey into the Grazi Kelly Universe today. You will find sassy, curvy heroines and sexy, love-driven heroes who find their HEAs between the pages. Werewolves, Bears, Dragons, Tigers, Witches, Romani,

Lynxes, Foxes, Thunderbirds, Vampires, and many more Shifters and supernatural creatures dwell within her worlds. The most important thing is every mate in this universe is fated, loyal, and true lovers always get their happily ever afters.

For a complete list of C.D. Gorri's books visit her website here: https://www.cdgorri.com/complete-book-list/

Thank you and happy reading!
del mare alla stella,
C.D. Gorri